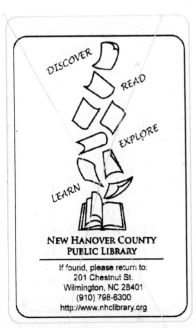

THE SHADOW
OF WHAT WE WERE

Luis Sepúlveda

THE SHADOW
OF WHAT WE WERE

*Translated from the Spanish
by Howard Curtis*

Europa
editions

Europa Editions
116 East 16th Street
New York, N.Y. 10003
www.europaeditions.com
info@europaeditions.com

Copyright © 2009 by Luis Sepúlveda
by arrangement with Literarische Agentur Mertin Inh.
Nicole Witt e. K., Frankfurt, Germany
First Publication 2011 by Europa Editions

Translation by Howard Curtis
Original Title: *La sombra de lo que fuimos*
Translation copyright © 2010 by Europa Editions

Library of Congress Cataloging in Publication Data is available
ISBN 978-1-60945-002-1

Sepúlveda, Luis
The Shadow of What We Were

Book design by Emanuele Ragnisco
www.mekkanografici.com

Prepress by Grafica Punto Print – Rome

Printed in Canada

To my comrades, male and female
who fell, and picked themselves up,
licked their wounds, cultivated their laughter,
preserved their gaiety, and carried on regardless.

"Not that it matters, but most of what follows is true."
—WILLIAM GOLDMAN, screenplay of
Butch Cassidy and the Sundance Kid

"I tell of many a notable thing,
Of people who obey no king,
Of enterprises high and bold
Fully deserving to be told."
—ALONSO DE ERCILLA Y ZUÑIGA,
La Araucana, canto I

THE SHADOW
OF WHAT WE WERE

1.

"All we old men have left now is Carlos Santana," the veteran thought, remembering another old man who had had the same idea forty years earlier—with the exception of one name—and had said it as he was being served a glass of wine.

"All we old men have left now is Carlos Gardel," his grandfather had sighed, looking nostalgically at the ruby-red wine. "Let's drink to his health."

That was all, the veteran remembered. The following day, his grandfather had blown his brains out with a .38-caliber Smith and Wesson special, the same gun he had kept for decades, well cleaned and lubricated, with the six bullets in the cylinder, wrapped in a piece of red and black felt resistant to damp, moths, and neglect.

That was how he had got it from Francisco Ascaso in a bar on Calle San Diego one rainy morning recorded on all the calendars in the world as July 16, 1925. There were two other men there, apart from Ascaso: Gregorio Jover and Buenaventura Durruti, the latter of whom complained about the Chilean wine, which he considered too sour, too rough on the belly, too sandpapery.

"Welcome to the ranks of the Just," he heard Durruti say. They clinked their glasses and Jover advised him to look after the revolver because it had a history. It was with that same weapon that Juan Soldevila y Romero, Cardinal Archbishop of Zaragoza, had been liquidated in 1923. "So be it," the veteran's grandfather replied. At the time, he was thirty years old, his name was Pedro Nolasco Arratia, and he worked for the Alvarado printing press, which specialized in calendars, veterinary almanacs, and books of verse by bards mourning imaginary love affairs. They finished the wine, paid, and took a taxi to the Matadero branch of the Bank of Chile.

This was the first bank robbery in the history of Santiago. According to witnesses, the four men entered with their faces uncovered, closed the one door, took out their weapons, and Durruti, in a voice more typical of a radio actor, said, "This is a robbery, but we're not thieves. The capitalists unite to exploit the peoples of the world, so it's only fair that we attack them where they least expect it. The money we're going to take will bring happiness to the wretched of the earth. Good health and anarchy!"

The following day, the newspaper *Ultima Hora* carried an interview with Luis Alberto Figueroa, a cashier in the bank, who declared that the robbery had been carried out by four men, all armed, but that at no moment had he felt any fear, since those fellows had inspired more confidence in him than the bank's usual customers, and Señora Rosa Elvira Cárcamo, who sold meat from a stand at the slaughterhouse, testified that the four men passed her establishment about ten minutes after committing the crime, just as she was placing a string of recently boiled blood sausages on the counter. Three of them spoke like Spaniards and one like a Chilean, Señora Cárcamo declared. The tallest of the Spaniards—Durruti, to judge from a photograph sent by the Argentine police—had exclaimed, on seeing the blood sausages, that they were superb, and the Chilean had told him that in Chile they were called *prietas* and that, served with spicy mashed potatoes, they were the best thing in the world. They bought four pounds of them, and, to pay, they took money from a bag in which, according to Señora Cárcamo, there was more money than a respectable man can earn through honest toil.

Another witness who crossed their path was a daily visitor to the slaughterhouse, the young poet Carlos Díaz Loyola, who signed his verses Pablo de Rokha. According to him, the robbers had paid for their purchases and walked away through the crowd as it considered the virtues of all those pork ribs seasoned in the Chillán style, those crepuscular miles of pork sausage, those positively Wagnerian braids of cow's intestines, those udders embellished with parsley, and those bull's testicles, which, when opened, exhibited all the virility of the Osorno breed.

It is worth mentioning that another poet, Ricardo Eliezer Neftalí Reyes Basoalto, better known in the bohemian circles of the time as Pablo Neruda, read this statement, and in a passionate letter to the editor of *Ultima Hora* criticized the bard from Alicante for his clear contempt toward udders. "Just as a woman's breasts do not merit the opprobrium of a gloved hand, udders should not be embittered with parsley, since there is nothing more worthy or sensual than the fragrant repose of celery."

In the same newspaper, Marco Antonio Salaberry, then head of the Criminal Investigation Department, expressed his surprise that the perpetrators, having committed such a terrible offence against property, had left the scene of the crime on foot, as naturally as worshippers leaving mass. He hoped that the criminals would soon be apprehended, while at the same time expressing his concern over a crime that was unheard of in a peaceful, law-abiding country.

"So," the veteran thought, "I'm the grandson of a pioneer." And before leaving home he looked at himself in the mirror. He was dressed entirely in black, his jacket loose enough not to show the bulge of the revolver under his left armpit. In his pockets, he had only a few coins and a sheet torn from a notebook with a telephone number on it.

"I am the shadow of what we were, and while there is light we will exist," he murmured before closing the door.

2.

Cacho Salinas hated chickens, hens, ducks, turkeys, and any creature that had feathers, but even so he stopped to look at the spit on which forty-odd broilers were turning, lined up in ranks like the robot soldiers in *Star Wars*.

"How are the chickens?" he asked the vendor, who was busy reading the sports pages of a newspaper.

"Stark naked and dead, what do you expect?" the man replied.

He hated chickens, not because of their taste, but because they were stupid and he blamed them for passing on a disease the first symptom of which was a lack of imagination. Lolo Garmendia had asked him to take care of the food for the group, and, when he e-mailed him to ask what he should buy, the answer was categorical: Buy chickens.

"Are the chickens fresh? Are they tasty? That's what I want to know."

The vendor closed his newspaper, glanced out at the street and then up at the ceiling of the shop. "Look, friend, I don't know where these chickens come from and I don't care, they're all the same, exactly the same weight, they come frozen, hard as rocks and glassy-eyed. I defrost them, stick skewers up their asses and out through the backs of their necks, smear them with a sauce that comes in a plastic bag, and after forty minutes on the spit they turn into something edible. Happy now? Don't make things any more complicated than they are."

Just then, it started to rain, gently at first, and then the storm broke, furiously pounding the corrugated iron roof. At last, Cacho Salinas thought, he had met a Chilean with a mind of his own and, better still, honest. Anyone else, in his place, would have smiled all over his face and praised his chickens to the skies. A woman entered, shaking her umbrella. She asked for a "nice" chicken, and, as she paid, complained about the chicken she had bought days earlier.

"It was nothing but skin and bones," she said.

"It was a diet chicken, señora," the vendor said as he handed over her purchase. "Haven't you heard about the anti-obesity campaign? Do you want your son to be a tub of lard like all those fat, lazy young black rappers in the Bronx?"

Cars rushed past in the rain as if escaping from something indefinable, and Cacho Salinas thought longingly of cities that glowed and glittered when it rained. One was Bilbao, full of welcoming places to take shelter; another was Gijón, where you could walk along the wall of San Lorenzo in a downpour; another was Hamburg, with its cobbled streets reflecting a myriad of lights. But Santiago couldn't be any sadder in the rain. He remembered reading Ramón Díaz Eterovic's novel *The City is Sad* during his exile in Paris, and, hunched over the book in La Petite Périgourdine, the bar in Saint-Michel that for some reason was popular with Latin Americans, weeping at the author's masterly description of the sadness of Santiago.

"I'll take six diet chickens. Can I stay here until the rain stops?"

The vendor indicated one of the three tables with their plastic covers, and left the cash desk, carrying a bottle of wine and two glasses. As he poured, the two men looked each other in the eyes for a brief moment and discovered the same shadows, the same bags under the eyes, the same historical glaucoma that allowed them to see parallel realities or to read existence as two narrative lines destined never to coincide: reality and desire. People who have survived the same shipwreck have a sixth sense that allows them to recognize one another, like dwarves.

"I'm sorry if I was rude to you earlier, but they piss me off all day long, either complaining about the chickens or asking me for their résumés. Let's have a drink and talk. Not even flies come in here when it rains. Cheers."

"You were honest with me, which is always a good thing. Cheers."

As they talked and sipped their wine, they discovered they were united by the same hatred for chickens and a similar problem with plucked birds.

The vendor had been, and still was, a Communist—it was like a moral wart you could never get rid of, he said. He, too, had returned from exile, in his case after ten years in Sweden. He sighed as he recalled Gothenburg, its islands, the steel-gray sea, and the women, who, according to him, freely and joyfully choose which man to share their Ikea bed with, and there's nothing you can do about it. He had two sons free of the burden of nostalgia, boys who had discovered Scandinavian roots, and, however vague they were, they were nevertheless roots that were slowly sinking into the rocky soil, boys who preferred jazz nights at the Nefertiti Bar to Latin American folk clubs, and who thrilled to the music of the group Psycore, because Kalle

Sepúlveda's guitar solos stirred them more than the plaintive melodies of Gitano Rodríguez.

In Gothenburg he had made friends with a number of Spanish émigrés who had arrived there in the 1960s to build the welfare state.

"They were good guys, those Andalusian construction workers, Asturian mechanics, Extremaduran laborers. They invited you to their houses, where there was never any shortage of Spanish omelet or ham worthy of the name. They all worked and saved with the same idea in mind: to go back to Spain and open a bar. It was an obsession with them, and whenever I was in their company it occurred to me that the reason El Cid went to Valencia was because he was planning to open a bar, and that if, in the rest of the world, the history of all existing society was the history of class struggle, in Spain it was the history of barkeepers and their customers, a factor overlooked by Marx and Engels, who, as philosophers, are very likely to have been teetotalers.

"Their enthusiasm rubbed off, and, when the dictatorship ended, my wife and I came back with the same idea. First of all we opened a little restaurant, a Scandinavian one, which didn't last long because it's impossible to convince Chileans that herrings aren't just cat food and that seafood isn't only eaten raw. I hope the Spaniards had better luck than me, and that they all own bars packed with thirsty people. We were ready to pack our bags and go back to Sweden when one day, inspired by 24-hour drugstores, some guys opened the first 24-hour liquor stores. So I decided to open a 24-hour chicken store, and here we are, roasting chickens while the earth turns on its axis. I hate chickens. Cheers, comrade, and tell me why *you* hate them so much."

"Another day," Cacho Salinas replied. "It's a long story, but I can assure you, my hatred of poultry is stronger than yours."

Carrying two plastic bags, he went back out on the street. The rain had eased a little, and he set off, surrounded by people hurrying past and cursing the climate of this country whose national anthem calls it, modestly, *the happy copy of Eden.*

3.

First there was the sound of broken glass, then the object hurtled through the window and struggled to climb a fraction of an inch, only to be immediately defeated by gravity and come plummeting to earth. The fall did not last more than a few seconds. If anyone had been looking up into the dark sky of Santiago at that moment and in that place, he would have seen an object that could easily have been taken for a small suitcase, with a cable coming out of the side like the tail of an animal that can't fly because of its totally non-aerodynamic shape and evident absence of wings.

When the object finally crashed to the ground, it opened in a final attempt at identity. It was one of the greatest technological wonders of the 1960s: a Dual phonograph that could play not only LPs and 45s but even those sentimental 78s. As it hit, the lid, which had been holding in the two speakers of the first stereophonic apparatus in the history of mankind, came off. The box of needles also came out from inside the machine, and the needles were strewn over the sidewalk like strange metal seeds sowed by the invisible humidity of nostalgia.

If, in its fall, the phonograph had not met with any resistance other than the damp air of a winter night, the impact would have been much greater. The geometric structure was not designed by its German engineers to support such shocks. Shaken by that atomic tremor, betrayed by its glue, its dovetail joint torn asunder, and the headless nails holding it together all flying off, it would have been nothing more than a lot of splinters scattered over the wet sidewalk. But the phonograph's fall was broken by the head of a man who, having the whole city to move about in, had chosen that street, that rainy night, and that moment of vertical doom.

He caught the blow, stopped in his tracks, staggered, was aware of the rain and the Santiago night fading out, leaned back against a wall, and, as his body slid down it, unable to overcome the pressing call of the ground, raised both hands to his head, looking for an answer that would never come, and finally fell on his side. There was an opening in his head, from which bubbles of blood escaped, along with the gray matter that had been hidden away for sixty-five years within its calcium casing.

Books fell on him, one after the other: *The Open Veins of Latin America* by Eduardo Galeano, *Notes from the Gallows* by Julius Fucik, *The Art of Loving* by Erich Fromm, and *Basic Concepts of Historical Materialism* by Marta Harnecker.

A further succession of objects would have covered that supine body if it had not been for the man who, in the middle of his struggle with a woman who was attempting to throw a pile of Quilapayún records through the shattered window, saw the fallen man, and lifted his hands to his mouth. The woman did the same, and then, still frozen in those gestures of astonishment, they looked at each other.

"You fucked up, Concha," the man muttered.

Concepción García collapsed into a ball, heedless of the drops of rain spattering her back. She paid no attention to her husband's observation that there wasn't a soul to be seen on the street, nor to his hand shaking her as he proposed going down to check if the man on the street was badly hurt.

Coco Aravena went out onto the landing and then set off down the four flights of stairs. "You fucked up," he kept muttering as he went downstairs. Only minutes earlier, everything had been fine, he'd been perfectly happy when he got back from the video store with a copy of *Reservoir Dogs* and a pack of beers, ready to spend a rainy night in the best way he knew: watching a classic, the best Tarantino ever, better than *Pulp Fiction*, as he had told his wife as soon as he opened the door, but Concha had virtually ignored him, instead brandishing a bundle of papers and announcing hysterically that they were being thrown out of their apartment because they were persistently behind in the rent.

"Calm down, Concha," he had pleaded, putting the beers in the icebox. "We have to keep calm." But she wouldn't let it go, she'd had all she could take, she said, of the shameless apathy and laziness of a man who didn't even bat an eyelid when confronted with evidence that they were about to be thrown out on the fucking street.

"Come on, Concha, let's keep calm, we can work it all out tomorrow, we have to be optimistic, think positive, smile, Conchita. Come on, sit down next to me and let's enjoy this gem I brought home, a classic, darling, a classic."

Before a volcano erupts, there is usually a series of small tremors that increase in intensity over a short period of time, and the muscular strength of the earth can be felt in the air. Something like that happened to Concepción García. Her facial muscles contracted, her clenched teeth chattered, her clenched fists clung to her body, and the eruption, verbal at first, centered on the fact that she'd had it up to here with his damned classics, that she was fed up living with a failure who didn't lift a finger to get out of poverty, a lazy man who never did anything but park his ass in the armchair and cry his eyes out over movies that didn't interest any human being with an ounce of sense, or maybe he hadn't been crying his eyes out the previous night while she was darning socks?

"No one can remain unmoved watching *The Man Who Shot Liberty Valance*," her husband replied in his defense. That was when the volcano erupted and Troy finally burned. The woman went to the cabinet, grabbed the phonograph, a true classic of technology, and saying, "There goes your classic of music," hurled it at the window, following that by grabbing the books, crying, "There go your classics of social literature," and hurling them, too, out onto the street, and he only managed to stop her as she was grabbing his classics of protest song.

Coco Aravena came out onto the street just as it was starting to rain really hard again. He looked right and left, was pleased to see that nobody was about, and walked over to the fallen man.

"Friend," he murmured, touching an arm, but the man, who was dressed entirely in black, did not respond.

He recalled how, in movies, they sometimes check to see if someone is still alive by touching his neck, but he couldn't bring himself to do it. And anyway, in movies they never showed you a close-up of the exact spot you had to touch, so instead he kicked the body a couple of times, which convinced him that the black-clad man was no longer of this earth.

Once again, he looked up and down the street. Emboldened by the fact that he was alone, he looked through the dead man's pockets. He found a handful of coins and a small sheet of paper. It was as he was trying to check the inside pockets of the jacket that he discovered the revolver in its leather shoulder holster.

"Oh, Concha!" he sighed. "You really blew it this time, you killed a cop."

And he started back home.

4.

Lucho Arancibia was doing the crossword in the Sunday supplement of *El Mercurio*, thinking how good it would have been at this hour in his parents' house, with the paraffin stove lit, watching TV in silence while his mother laid the table for dinner and announced that, as they often did on rainy days, they had hard fritters for dessert.

"It's strange," he said to himself. "*El Mercurio* is a Chilean newspaper, but they never put in the crossword: seven-letter word, fried pancake made with wheat flour and boiled pumpkin pulp, fritter, or two words meaning a dessert made with fried pancakes of wheat flour, boiled pumpkin pulp, soaked in syrup of sugar cane, better known as wheat cake, *ergo*, hard fritter."

It was cold in the garage, and the rain pounding on the zinc roof merely added to the feeling of neglect that hung over the place. A dust-covered hydraulic jack and a tire changer spoke of days gone by, when they had worked at the noble mission of setting back into motion what life had brought to a halt.

Pitica Ubilla, the Chilean striptease queen, still hung on the plasterboard wall, showing off her monumental breasts, albeit half-covered by a sequined bra. She was the subject of the last calendar produced by the Arancibia brothers' garage.

Arancibia Brothers, Top Mechanics, he read aloud, and it seemed to him that he could hear the hustle and bustle of the good old days, when he and Juan and Alberto had worked hard at repairing whatever old clunkers had come their way. He looked around and discovered that, in addition to the jack and the tire changer, there was also an oil drum converted into a grill.

He went back to the crossword. Six letters, city in Basque country.

"Bilbao, they always do that one. Why don't they put intelligent words that have some connection to us? For example: Ten letters, concentration camp where, if they took you out at night, you never came back. Puchuncaví. Ten letters, how you feel when your parents visit you in prison and tell you your brother Juan's body has been found on a garbage dump riddled with bullets. Devastated. Seven letters, how you feel when you make a hole in the ground and find three skeletons with their hands tied behind their backs and one of them is wearing your brother Alberto's shoes. Furious. Shit, I'm talking to myself again."

A few knocks at the door jolted him from his crossword. He stood up, half opened, and saw a very wet man hugging two plastic bags.

"Password," he demanded.

"It's me, Cacho Salinas. Open up, the chickens are getting wet."

"Tell me the password or I won't open," he insisted.

"Lucho, it's me, you idiot," Salinas implored, dripping water. "There's no password, that was before, we're not underground anymore, all that's over now."

"He's like my left testicle," Lolo Garmendia had said, referring to the man still standing there impassively on the other side of the door. "Those bastards messed with his head, but he's still hard at work. Just try to go with the flow."

"I don't remember the password. Give me a clue."

"Marching song we used to sing in the Young Communist training school. First line of the first verse."

Salinas transferred both bags to his left hand and pressed his right hand to his forehead. "*From the deep crucible of the fatherland . . .*"

"No. That's the first verse of *Venceremos*, and we never sang it in the training school. I'm not opening."

"Look at me, I'm Cacho Salinas, older but still the same, and I'm soaking wet, you damned idiot."

"You can't come in without the password. But I'll give you another clue. Marching song that used to be sung by the comrades of the Komsomol, with words by the French poet Gaston Montéhus."

Salinas felt like kicking the door, turning around and taking off, but then what would he do with the chickens? He closed his eyes and racked his neurons until the little red proletarian songbook appeared on the screen of his mind. It couldn't be the *Internationale* or *La Varsoviana*. Then he remembered that the man on the other side of the door used to be called Luis Pavel, after Pavel Korchagin, the hero of *How The Steel Was Tempered*.

"*We are the young guard*," Salinas crooned.

"*We are building the future*," Arancibia joined in, and opened the door.

Cacho Salinas entered, took off his soaked overcoat, left the bag with the roast chickens on a large plasterboard table, and, on seeing the half drum converted into a grill, suggested they look for some sticks to light a fire.

"Sit down, I'll do it," Arancibia replied, and he walked toward a corner piled high with junk, singing in a husky voice, "*Children of poverty, which made us rebels.*" Salinas saw him poking about in the junk. Arancibia was still well-built, but just as the Santiago that lay on the other side of the door wasn't the city he remembered, so this Lucho Arancibia wasn't the strong young man who had enthused the others when they did voluntary work back in the 1960s, when Communist girls would tie red scarves around the necks of their male comrades and kiss them as a foretaste of love in the days still to come. "*We are the sons of Lenin, tremble in your boots, our hammer and our sickle will pull you up by the roots.*"

He threw a bundle of dry sticks on the half drum, crumpled a few pages of the Sunday supplement of *El Mercurio,* lit the fire, and continued singing as he watched the flames growing.

"*Early in the morning, the masses will arise, the red guard will go marching, shaking the earth with their cries.*"

"How's it going, red guard?" Salinas said, offering him a cigarette.

"What can I say?" Arancibia replied, raising a lighted firelighter to it. "We aren't the Young Guard anymore."

No. They weren't the Young Guard. Their youth had been scattered in hundreds of places, burned by electric prods during interrogations, buried in secret graves that were slowly being discovered, in years of prison, in strange rooms in even stranger countries, in Homeric returns to nowhere, and all that was left were the marching songs that nobody sang anymore because those in charge now had decided that there had never been young people like them in Chile, that no one had ever sung *The Young*

Guard, and that the Communist girls had not had the taste of the future on their lips.

"You ought to take the chickens out," Arancibia said. "They get all runny in plastic bags."

It was still raining over Santiago. The downpour had subsided to a persistent shower, but very soon the clouds would be unleashing their fury again. The two men moved chairs closer to the fire and sat there watching the flames.

"Would you like a glass of wine?" Arancibia said. "I bought a bottle of Santa Rita. Lolo said I shouldn't bring wine, but I told him to go to hell, you have to drink wine at times like this."

"A drop of wine will go down very well in this weather," Salinas assured him.

They drank in silence. The Santa Rita was the same as ever, vigorous, strong, sour, rough on the belly, dry, sand-papery, but it warmed you up inside.

"It's been a long time," Salinas said.

"A very long time," Arancibia replied. "You left the Young Communists in '68."

"I didn't leave, Lucho. They expelled me along with hundreds of militants. Don't you remember when Che died in Bolivia? We didn't like what the Party said about him, that he was an irresponsible adventurer, a provocateur, a CIA agent. Many of us demonstrated our disagreement, and the Party responded with an act of faith in the Cine Nacional, the old movie theater on Avenida Independencia. There, the poisonous Don César Godoy Urrutia had his day of glory expelling hundreds of militants accused of ultra-leftism, the infantile disease of Communism. They ordered us to give up our membership cards and we threw them in the air, then they demanded that we take off our red scarves and no one did. I still have mine."

"Old times, dead times. I also wanted to leave, but I had to think of my parents, who had known Luis Emilio Recabarren and Elías Laferte, and my brothers Juan and Alberto who were party officials. In my family, you were a Communist or your name wasn't Arancibia. When did you come back from exile?"

He would have liked to reply that you never come back from exile, that however hard you try it's an illusion, an absurd attempt to live in a land you have kept in your memory. Everything is beautiful in the land of memory, nothing bad ever happens in the land of memory, there are no quakes and even the rain is pleasant in the land of memory. The land of memory is Neverland.

"About six months ago. I lived in Paris for thirteen years, and one day I told myself I had to come back."

"Paris. Did you meet Brigitte Bardot?"

"No. Why should I have met Brigitte Bardot?"

"I can't understand how you could have lived all those years in Paris and not met Brigitte Bardot. It doesn't make any sense."

"And what about you? Are you married, divorced, separated?"

"I talk to myself, Cacho," Arancibia said. "The soldiers messed with my head. Sometimes I'm walking along the street and I start arguing with myself. People look at me, some of them burst out laughing, others express pity, but I don't care. What woman would hitch up with a guy who talks to himself? So let me say now, if I suddenly start talking without anybody asking me anything, give me a slap, you have my permission. A slap in the face, just one. They messed with my head, but I'm not an idiot. What's keeping Lolo? He has to be here for when the specialist comes."

"Do you know anything about this guy?"

"Only that he's a specialist," Arancibia said, and he wanted to know what had intimidated Cacho, what had prevented him from getting to Brigitte Bardot. First of all, Salinas said, he hadn't had time, and besides, Brigitte Bardot was now a fat, reactionary, grouchy old woman who spent her time breeding dogs.

"You're lying," Arancibia replied. "She's gorgeous and blonde and sunbathes in the nude on the terrace, and to get to her you just have to push your way through the sheets hanging out to dry."

Immutable land of memory. As incorruptible as one of Saint Theresa's breasts or a movie by Roger Vadim.

5.

Concepción García did not bat an eyelid. She still sat curled up on the floor, while her husband took down the two parts of the broken window in the living room and replaced them with others from the bedroom. She sat there with her head bowed and her arms crossed over her chest, oblivious to Coco Aravena's frenzied attempts at repair, while he kept repeating, like some absurd self-help manual, that they had to stay calm. Concepción was a long way away from this wintry city and the recent homicide. She was in Berlin, happily walking along the Kurfürstendamm, looking at the shop windows, thinking she might go up to the cafeteria in the Hertie department store and treat herself to ice cream in a cup and look out at the roofs of the city, which, when it had welcomed her, had still had the feel of an island. She loved the cafeteria at the Hertie, the smell of coffee, tobacco and vanilla that pervaded the place. As soon as she had taken her first taste of the ice cream, an attentive waitress would come up to her and ask her *Na, schmeckt?* and she would reply, yes, she liked it, it was delicious. *Danke schön*, she would add with genuine emotion, because she loved living in a city where people cared about each other. Then she would go to a fruit shop, where she would marvel once again at the fruit so temptingly laid out, and she would hear a woman like her say, *Ich hätte gern zwei wunderschönen Tomaten*, and when her turn came she, too, would say, "I'd like two wonderful tomatoes," and the vendor would hand them to her with the words *Zwei wunderschönen Tomaten für die hübsche Dame*, and she would walk away happy to know that she was a pretty lady with two wonderful tomatoes. She had loved Berlin ever since the day when, together with her husband, who had insisted on sleeping throughout the flight, they had landed at Templehof and two young, extremely blond young men who could have been the sons she had never had embraced her and cried, "Welcome to Berlin, comrade!"

She had loved Berlin with a Kennedyesque intensity. After two weeks of attending an intensive German course given by volunteers of the *Chile Komite* she had gone for a walk with one of her teachers, a twenty-year-old named Helga who knew everything there was to know about Chile. They had come to the Wall. There, on the other side, was real socialism, protected by tons of concrete, electrified wire fencing, and a minefield. Helga told her they were at the Brandenburg Gate. In this very spot, she said, John F. Kennedy had uttered the famous words *Ich bin ein Berliner*. Then Concepción García climbed on a bench, opened her arms and exclaimed *Ich bin eine Berlinerin!* And Helga hugged her and said, "Yes, of course, you're a woman of Berlin."

"Concha? Did you understand what I said?"

She hadn't understood, she hadn't even been listening, hadn't noticed when he had squatted down in front of her.

"Could you repeat it, please?"

"The first thing to do is to keep calm. Calm. Two people came along the street and saw the dead man, so it's likely they've already informed the police, who are sure to come soon and ask questions. By my calculation, that'll be tomorrow, once they've found our fingerprints on the phonograph and the books. Do you understand?"

"What fingerprints?"

"Oh, Concha! If you paid attention to those classic crime movies, you'd know we leave our fingerprints and our DNA on everything we touch, and that's how they track down the killers."

Killers. So that was what she had become, a killer. Concepción García bit her lips and closed her eyes, trying in vain to disappear into a life-saving darkness.

"But we have to keep calm," her husband continued. "The first thing we'll do is go to the police station and report a robbery. Now this is the official version. We went to the video store together because we'd been waiting two weeks for them to get the Tarantino classic *Reservoir Dogs* back in. I went into the store, you stayed outside because you like the rain, and when we got back with the movie, alibi number one, we found the door open and we immediately noticed that the phonograph and other valuable objects were missing. We have to keep to this story, Concha. There are bound to be two police officers. One will be a brute and the other a nice guy, but that's just the old good cop bad cop routine. We have to stay calm and keep to our story."

Concepción García let him put her coat and woolen hat on her, and accepted his hand as they walked down the stairs, fervently hoping that she would come out onto Jakobstrasse, that it was a bright day in Kreuzberg with the smell of spices from the Turkish stores and the doner kebabs roasting slowly on vertical grills.

The rain was still falling, and the body was still on the sidewalk. His black clothes shone wetly, but there wasn't the slightest sign of either the lethal phonograph or the books.

"Fucking people," Coco Aravena muttered.

"What do you mean?" the woman said. "I don't understand what you're talking about."

"Look, Concha," Coco replied, pointing to the dead man's bare, marble-like feet. "They stole his shoes."

6.

In 1971, as soon as Allende assumed the presidency, the far left began to encourage occupations of workplaces. In many cases, the problems in these places, when examined closely, were no more than local difficulties that could have been settled easily and lawfully. But under the Leninist slogan "the worse the better," factories without the slightest importance were nevertheless occupied. As the popular government could not, of course, go in for repression, supervisors were appointed, recruited from among the militants, comrades who really understood the nature and limitations of a government of the people. The supervisors had to get all these occupied factories and small industries back to work as soon as possible. They had to be very dynamic and creative: being creative was the order of the day. To avoid bureaucratic delays, each supervisor was a representative of the Ministries of Labor, Social Welfare, Public Works, Agriculture, and even the Comrade President himself.

"They were people's commissars," Arancibia pointed out. "Like Strelnikov, that character in *Doctor Zhivago* with his armored train."

"Something like that," Salinas agreed, "but we didn't send any Turks to Siberia."

"Omar Sharif isn't Turkish," Arancibia said. "He's Egyptian."

"Will you let me carry on, or shall I give you a slap?"

"Carry on, but you have to be precise about historical details, otherwise you confuse the masses. More wine?"

"All right. The thing is, one day I was appointed supervisor of a poultry farm in Puente Alto, you know, to the south of Santiago. There were these wire mesh pens containing incubators that produced two thousand chickens a week, ugly white creatures, almost albinos, who were ready to be sacrificed after sixty days. In addition, the poultry farm had two thousand laying hens, which meant sixty thousand eggs were produced a month. It was a thriving concern, there were about twenty guys working there who really knew their jobs, and there was no problem in selling the products, so I settled in what had been the administrator's office with my sleeping bag and my books and my rucksack, and started familiarizing myself with the chickens and hens. Everything went well for the first two months, but in the third month, some comrades from the far left decided to occupy the food factory and we had no feed for the animals. The chickens and the hens held out for two days without appearing too upset, but on the third day the chickens began pecking at each other, the hens stopped laying, and it was heartbreaking to hear them clucking with hunger. As the order was to be creative, on the fifth day I went to the nearby fruit drying plant, which was also occupied, and where there were about fifty acres of fruit trees and a lot of grass, and the supervisor there gave me permission to bring my chickens and hens and let them graze. The workers on the poultry farm became shepherds, and it was quite a sight, seeing those ten thousand chickens and two thousand hens walking along a dirt track. But the country there is full of creepy-crawlies, fat snails, juicy earthworms, tasty crickets, and those hens and chickens had never seen a worm, didn't know anything about them, took fright, and ran away. They didn't even look at the pasture. The return journey to the farm was really sad, and what came next was even worse, because all that exercise had made them even hungrier and those damned chickens began to practice cannibalism.

"By the tenth day, only half the chickens were still alive, the hens weren't laying but were holding on, and, incredible as it now seems, one of them, one single hen, laid her regulation egg every day. I noted in my production report: eggs, one."

"She was a hen with class consciousness," Arancibia said.

"A heroine of socialist labor. On the eleventh day, torn between suicide and mass murder, we plumped for the latter. As being creative was the order, I gathered together the toughest-looking men on the poultry farm, and we armed ourselves with shotguns and set off for the food factory in a couple of trucks."

"That's what I call will. The kind of will shown by the Komsomols when they had to get coal to Moscow in the winter of 1919. The Atamans were hoping to use the cold as a tactic to defeat the Bolsheviks, they thought the winter would be on their side, would be their general, but they hadn't reckoned with the young guard, who all had the spirit of Pavel Korchagin. But there's one thing that bothers me. Those men who took over the food factory were comrades, too, and you can't resolve contradictions among the people with guns."

"Do you want a slap? Yes, they were comrades, but so were the guys who occupied vineyards and decided to drink all the wine themselves, claiming that they'd spent years sipping leftovers."

"Stalin said objective perception is impaired by class prejudice. Some of us were thirsty for justice, others for social equality, why shouldn't those guys have been thirsty for good wine? The petty bourgeoisie don't appreciate it. Carry on about the chickens."

"I'll remember that petty bourgeoisie remark, you idiot. We got to the factory, the first exchange of views wasn't very fraternal, and by the time we'd gotten through our inventory of insults we were quits. They were armed with shotguns and a few pistols and had no intention of letting us have a few bags of feed. We had our weapons and every intention of attacking the storerooms. But we reached an agreement in the end. They'd let us load our trucks if we sent them chickens to maintain their soup kitchen."

"The classes can reach temporary tactical agreements that don't hamper the strategy of the vanguard," Arancibia commented. "Lenin said that in *What Is to Be Done?*"

"Lenin knew nothing about chickens," Salinas replied, "and Comrade Nadezhda Krupskaya couldn't even fry an egg. According to Lenin himself in *The Stubborn Facts.*"

"It was a despicable act. You should have brought it before a committee of party officials, but as Comrade Vo Nguyen Giap said, however hard the bourgeoisie tries to falsify it, history always sides with the oppressed, and Comrade Alexandra Kollontai denounced the evil of social myths becoming obstacles to the freedom of love. I don't know what you're waiting for to finish your story. I want to know what happened to your damned chickens."

"Kollontai. Uttering her name was like mentioning Trotsky in front of Stalin, or Vietnam in the presence of

Nixon. We quickly loaded the trucks, drove back to the farm, dumped as much as we could in the feeding troughs, and I went off to sleep. I didn't sleep long, because a few hours later I was woken by one of the comrades who said the hens and chickens were having an orgy in the pens. To put it in the jargon you like so much, the creatures were engaged in the most bourgeois of liberalisms, and all because of us. In our haste, instead of loading the trucks with feed, we'd loaded them with bags containing a vitamin complex normally given in the ratio of one handful for every two bags of feed. The chickens were in a frenzy, and the hens had gone mad and were losing their plumage in handfuls. By dawn, we had seven thousand stark naked birds shivering with cold."

"Nothing matters if you're warmed by the great proletarian truths," Arancibia said.

"Bullshit. The only remedy was to approach the union at the copper wire factory. Those guys were the most sensible in the country. You remember old Yáñez? He put us in contact with the supervisor of a factory making heaters. We ended up surrounding the pens with gas heaters. I tell you, those were the most expensive eggs and chickens ever produced. I hate them with all my heart." By way of conclusion, Salinas emptied his glass in one gulp.

"Breast or thigh?" Arancibia asked, pulling apart one of the roast chickens.

"Careful," Salinas replied. "Just one spark can set a meadow on fire."

7.

The headquarters of the Criminal Investigation Department was opposite a red brick building they were starting to demolish. This building had formerly been a prison, an example of Turinese baroque architecture, Chilean style, which during its time as a prison had had nothing to envy Alcatraz as a university of crime.

From his office, Inspector Crespo watched the rain falling, hoping that it would clear up before daybreak. But the weather forecast had predicted more rain over Santiago, and he couldn't help laughing when he thought of the working class districts, where, at that hour, the usual crooks would be blocking the drains with garbage. That way, the streets would be turned into fast-flowing rivers, and the inheritors of that criminal underworld that had arrived with the conquistadors would be on the corners, dressed in plastic raincoats and rubber boots, offering their services as packhorses. In return for a few pesos, they would carry those city-dwellers who didn't want to get wet from one side of the street to the other. On one occasion, he had come across a group of men who were blocking the drains and had accused them of committing a criminal act.

The men had not batted an eyelid. Claiming it was a free market, they had carried on with their mission of turning Santiago into a sad replica of Venice.

At that moment, Detective Adela Bobadilla entered, proud to be part of the first generation of police officers with clean hands, those who weren't even born yet in 1973 or were too young to be torturers or the allies of drug traffickers. She was soaking wet. She took off her blue oilskin, hung it next to the heater, and responded to the inspector's "What's cooking?" by handing him some sheets of paper.

"Read it to me," the inspector said. "You have a nice voice and I like to be told stories when it's raining."

"We have a body found on the street. Male, about seventy years old, six feet tall, 210 pounds, wearing black pants, a black T-shirt, and a black jacket—and he was barefoot."

"Had he been walking around barefoot or did he simply not have any shoes when he was found?"

"I don't know, inspector. He had a wound on the head, caused by a blunt instrument with sharp edges. Probable cause of death: fracture of the right parietal, with loss of brain matter and hemorrhaging. He had no ID on him, but we got a positive result from the fingerprints."

"The only positive result would have been if the poor guy was still alive."

"His name is Pedro Nolasco Gonzalez," Detective Bobadilla said, and broke off when she saw the inspector suddenly freeze. She was familiar with that gesture: like a cat startled into alertness.

"Ask for a patrol car and put your uniform back on," the inspector said. "We're going to the morgue."

With the rain falling outside, the warmth of the patrol car was conducive to sitting back and asking the driver to take them somewhere, anywhere. Detective Bobadilla was waiting for the inspector to open his mouth. His furrowed brows indicated that his brain was working overtime.

"I suppose you looked at his criminal record."

"Yes, inspector. If you can call it a criminal record. It's a long list, all relating to minor but unusual offences. The last thing we have on him is that in 1982 he's reported to have attacked a mink farm in Patagonia, released about two thousand of the animals, valued at several hundred thousand pesos, and the animals then mixed with the local fauna and lost all their value. The crime was reported by some furriers related by marriage to General Arellano."

"And the whole of Chile was in fits of laughter when the thing came out. As you're very young, Adelita, and they taught you history from a two-page pamphlet, you don't know that at the time of the military government— the authoritarian regime, as those who've banished the word dictatorship from the dictionary call it—Pinochet gave the country to a son-in-law of his, a delinquent with a name that sounded like cough syrup, Ponce-Leroux, as a reward for marrying his dumbest daughter. That's nothing new. In every country, those who agree to take on the stupid offspring of the rich and powerful get something in return, so why should Chileans be any different? Today, that son-in-law is one of the richest men in the world, having made his fortune buying national industries at fire sale prices and selling them later for an untold profit. It must have been hard, having to share a bed with that dumb girl and her hairy legs, but as compensation he received the southern forests and turned them into splinters. One day, a group of army officers, upset at the prices their wives were paying for furs in the stores of Miami, gave him the task of promoting fur production in Chile, and he imported thousands of Canadian minks and put them on farms in Patagonia. But he hadn't reckoned with Patagonian rabbits, sex maniacs that'll mount anything that moves. The species degenerated, with some of the minks being born with long ears and pompoms on their asses. It turned into a real plague, and they had to be shot. I would have given him a medal."

"In 1998 he was reported for committing an outrage against the salmon fisheries at Puerto Aysén."

"Another act more worthy of gratitude than punishment. Do you know why fish is so expensive? Because our economists handed over the southern fjords to foreign companies. To produce one pound of salmon, in addition to hormones and colorants you need nine pounds of fish converted into feed, which we, being a generous country and a leader in free trade, provide gratis. It was never proved that Nolasco was with the ecological group that climbed over the dikes and released thousands of salmon."

"The strangest of all is that there's still an arrest warrant from 1971, but there's no indication of the crime, and the warrant hasn't expired."

"You were born in '73, weren't you, Adelita?" Detective Bobadilla nodded, and the inspector put his hands together, like a grandfather about to tell a story about Pedro Urdemales.

"Three years before you came into the world, Salvador Allende won the presidential election, and one year later, in June 1971, an organization called the Organized Vanguard of the People, made up of anarchists and members of the underclass, assassinated a former minister in the previous government, Señor Edmundo Pérez Zujovic.

This minister had been responsible for a massacre in Puerto Montt of men and women who had illegally occupied some land to build shacks where they could spend the treacherously cold southern winter. I was young then, as you are now, and had only just graduated from the police academy. The order came down from higher up: Find the minister's assassins and kill them. Who gave the order? Maybe one day history will tell us, the day we Chileans stop being wimps afraid of our own past. The assassins were two brothers named Rivera Calderón. First, their sister was tracked down and tortured into betraying her brothers, then they were found and liquidated. A few weeks later, another OVP militant, an old man named Heriberto Salazar Bello, approached this building with explosives hidden under his coat, waited for the new shift to arrive, and blew himself up. The explosion killed three officers who were just going on duty. The case ended up with one person still on the run. That person was Pedro Nolasco González, although it was never proved beyond a doubt that he was connected with the assassination of the former minister."

"So why the arrest warrant?" Detective Bobadilla asked.

"Because we're an unforgiving country. Back in 1925, Pedro Nolasco González's grandfather, who was also called Pedro, robbed a bank along with three Spanish anarchists."

"The famous Bank of Chile job, the first of its kind in the country?"

"That's right, Adelita. Except for one thing. The first bank robbery in Chilean history was actually committed by a gang of American bandits in Punta Arenas. On December 20, 1905, Etta Place, Butch Cassidy and the

Sundance Kid robbed the Bank of London and Tarapaca and got away with a thousand gold pesos. *O tempora, o mores!*"

The veteran's corpse was in a steel tray covered with a green canvas sheet. A label had been attached to the big toe of his right foot, which the inspector read before lifting the sheet.

"Tough luck, Pedrito," the inspector murmured. "To end up like this, with all your ideas escaping through a hole. What do you think, Adelita?"

"Well, it's obvious the blow killed him."

"Adelita, the man was six feet tall and in spite of his age was still well-built. To give him such a strong blow, the killer would have had to be about six foot five, and there aren't many people who could play for the Lakers in this country. I incline more to the idea of an accidental death, a falling flowerpot, for instance. Did they find anything like that near the body?"

"No, inspector, but a couple living on the street where he was found reported a theft of electrical appliances."

The inspector asked for a magnifying glass and carefully examined the wound. Then he asked for a pair of tweezers, poked about in the dead man's right ear, and extracted a thin strip of metal.

"Do you enjoy listening to music, Adelita?"

"Yes, inspector. In my spare time, of course."

"And how do you listen to it?"

"Well, I have a CD player, and an MP3."

"Let me introduce you to a piece of musical archaeology. A phonograph needle."

Detective Bobadilla placed the object in a small plastic bag and asked what they were going to do next.

"The most sensible thing we can do is look for a place where we can get a decent cup of tea and some hard fritters. I can't think of anything better when it's raining."

That was when Detective Bobadilla realized that it was going to be a long night.

8.

Lolo Garmendia left the bag of bread next to the chickens, took off his dripping wet raincoat, and met Cacho Salinas's gaze. He could imagine what the other man must be thinking, seeing him at least sixty pounds heavier, a couple of pounds for every year they had been apart. And bald, too, stripped forever of that Black Panther mop that used to draw sighs from the female comrades. But the man in front of him had changed, too, and wasn't the same person he had given a farewell hug that Tuesday, September 11, 1973.

"Damn it, Lolo, we're so old," Salinas said in greeting.

"And you with that Santa Claus beard," Garmendia replied, and the two men joined in an embrace.

If life was a screenplay, the writer ought to make sure that when people met, there shouldn't be any perceptible changes—as the poet Juan Gelman put it, *the years grow old with me*—and there shouldn't be any of those doubts that reason refuses to accept, blaming the innocent eye for the truth it sees in front of it. Those two men clapping each other on the back had been friends, they'd been part of the same gang, addicted to soccer, politics and weekend barbecues. They had fully intended to continue their friendship, to keep it intact as the years passed. They had been comrades, working together to make their country if not a better place, at least a less boring one, until that rainy September morning arrived. From noon onwards, the clocks had started to strike unknown hours, hours of mistrust, hours when friendships faded and disappeared, and all that remained was the terrified wailing of widows and mothers. Life became riddled with black holes. They were everywhere, you went into a subway station and never came out, you got into a taxi and never reached home, you talked of light and were swallowed up by shadows.

Many friends and acquaintances denied knowing one another, in an epidemic of amnesia that was essential for self-preservation. No, I don't know those guys who've just been thrown in the back of a truck and driven away. No, I've never seen that woman who's waiting on the corner.

Forgetting became a pressing need, you had to cross to the other side of the street to avoid meeting, or turn around quickly and retrace your steps. And everything that had been pregnant with the future suddenly became poisoned with the past.

"Hugging for more than a minute means you're gay," Arancibia said, handing the newcomer a glass of wine.

"I said no alcohol," Garmendia pointed out, accepting the glass.

"I brought it," Salinas said. "These fucking chickens don't go down well with water. Cheers."

They drank in silence, while the rain lashed the roof.

Lucho Arancibia was here because he still owned the garage, and because after many days of talking to Lolo Garmendia, Lolo had convinced him of what he already knew: that there was no such thing as justice and only fools or cowards could believe that one day the paternal handkerchief of the State would dry all the tears that had been wept or held in for more than thirty years now.

As for Cacho Salinas, he was principally here because his chance contact with Garmendia had distracted him from his solitude, from wandering like a zombie through the streets of Santiago and stopping by a phone booth, already lacking the willpower to dial the prefix for France and then the number of a telephone that stood on an unknown table in a strange house and—if he was lucky and Matilde answered—hear the same frosty voice urging him to sort out his life, and to please understand that she had someone else now. Until his contact with Garmendia, he would visit internet cafés to chat for a few minutes with his son in Brussels, getting back those voiceless words inviting him to meet his grandson, born two years earlier.

One afternoon, as he was searching for the online edition of *Le Monde*, he found himself by mistake on a page full of ads, and, amid the profusion of offers involving every known sex and position, he came across an ad that sent a shiver down his spine.

"NLA. Vizcachas Column. Contact." Next to it was the address of a social networking site. He clicked on it, registered, and what he then read left him even more amazed. "If you were a comrade in the Vizacachas Column, reply to this. Blackpanther."

He was pleased to discover that Lolo Garmendia was still alive. They had both left the Young Communists to join the ranks of the Socialists, and were soon active in the strongest faction of the party, the National Liberation Army, an internationalist tendency that, while considering the armed struggle a possible means of achieving power, nevertheless recognized that Chile was a special case, a peaceful country in a continent that reeked of gunpowder. The Chilean NLA had come into being to support the struggle begun by Che in Bolivia.

Sitting there in front of the computer in the internet café, he saw images on the screen that only he could see. He saw himself with Garmendia under that brillo pad of Jimi Hendrix hair hearing the news of the death in the mountains of Bolivia of the journalist Elmo Catalán, and of the police officer Tirso Molina and the boxing champion Agustín Carrillo, members of the Chilean NLA who had died in the Bolivian war. He also saw himself at Garmendia's side, defending the reservoir that provided Santiago with drinking water when the Fascists of the Fatherland and Freedom movement tried to blow them up, and on the morning of September 11, 1973, together with other NLA members, shooting their way toward the palace of La Moneda. Allende was holding out there, together with NLA comrades in the presidential guard, the GAP, plus a handful of police officers who had remained loyal to him.

They didn't manage to get within ten blocks of La Moneda. They were on their way to an appointment with death, but death was too busy and paid no attention to them.

Later, as the months and years passed, they learned that Allende and the GAP comrades had fought until they ran out of ammunition. Even though confronted with a well-armed enemy that outnumbered them a hundred to one, they caused numerous casualties, and the only two defenders of La Moneda who had died were Allende's best friend, the journalist Augusto Olivares, and the president himself. Both had committed suicide.

In accordance with Allende's last instructions, the GAP comrades surrendered. They were disarmed and handed over to the Chilean army and its torturers, who didn't give a damn for the Geneva Convention. Never did an army dishonor itself as they did.

Salinas answered the message, leaving the telephone number of the boarding house where he was living, and waited for a reply. On the third day he went back to the internet café, searched again for the ad, and found a very brief text: "No phones, below is my e-mail address, open a hotmail account with your old nickname."

"I assumed you were somewhere in South America, or the Caribbean," Garmendia said. "I never forgot that whenever you talked about the future, you always said you saw yourself in a place with a beach, drinking, fishing, eating, fucking and smoking, all those gerunds of yours. I was surprised when I read your reply."

"I did some of that," Salinas replied, "but Chilean style, a little of everything. I never heard any more about you, though I left the Party in the eighties. What happened after we said goodbye?"

"I stayed in Santiago for a while. It was tough, the safe houses were disappearing one after another, and in the end it was Lucho's family that saved me. Good people, brave people. Although Lucho's two brothers had both been arrested, they took me in and hid me until I was able to leave the country. When I was in exile, I found out they'd both been murdered."

"I'm sorry, Lucho, I didn't know," Salinas said.

"In the words of Comrade Lenin," Arancibia said, pouring more wine, "we men cannot correct the events of the past, but we can anticipate the events of the future."

Garmendia took a sip, proposed throwing a few more logs on the fire, and then told them how he had arrived in Buenos Aires in the midst of the conflict between the Montoneros, the People's Revolutionary Army, Triple A, and right-wing commandos. "It was a difficult dance," he said, "you never knew who to dance with and the music was quite sad."

"That's where he started going bald," Arancibia remarked. "With that lion's mane, he was a perfect target."

"I'm not so sure of that. If you want to know when I started to lose my hair, I'll tell you. From Argentina, thanks to some bastard official in the High Commission for Refugees, they sent me to Romania, the Carpathian land ruled over by Comrade Nicolae Ceausescu, the titan of titans, and his wife Elena, the fairy godmother of fairy godmothers.

"For an exile, Romanian socialism was paradise, but the kind of paradise the priests told us about in Chile, a place where you arrive, sit down on a cloud, and play the harp for all eternity. That's what I did. I arrived, they took away all my papers for reasons of security and assigned me a guardian angel, a short man with a thick mustache and a garlic-based diet. His name was Constantinescu, and he was a Securitate officer whose mission was to be with me twenty-four hours a day and report back on everything I did. The first thing I saw when I woke up in the morning was Comrade Constantinescu. While I brushed my teeth, he would check the pillow, the mattress and the blankets, looking for something without even knowing what he was looking for. Then I was expected to study the works of Comrade Nicolae until noon, and continue in the afternoon with the works of Comrade Elena, philosopher, economist, astrologer and obstetrician, all rolled into one. On Sundays, to keep everyone happy, I had to go to the theater and listen to poems by Comrade Nicolae about Comrade Nicolae, or watch a play about some heroic act of the titan of titans, the victor of all wars, the infallible strategist and distinguished marshal.

"If I didn't weep enough at the sufferings of Comrade Nicolae, Comrade Constantinescu noted it down in a little book and looked at me as if to say, I caught you, you traitor. If I didn't applaud until my hands hurt after hearing a poem by Comrade Elena, he'd do the same.

"I don't remember exactly when it was, but it was definitely during a play extolling the maternal love of Elena Ceausescu, mother of all Romanians and virgin of virgins, that I lifted my hand to my head and for the first time when I took it away found it was full of hair.

"Comrade Constantinescu made a note of it, took a handful of hair from me, and put it in a little plastic bag with the unmistakable Securitate seal. I was so used to his being there that I didn't pay any attention, but when I left the theater I didn't see him. I got worried, and started looking for him, in four years you get used to someone, and your spy becomes your soul brother, I even called out his name in that desolate, cold Bucharest of the mid-eighties. My guardian angel had disappeared, so I started walking and by the time I was in the vicinity of the Gara de Nord I felt like eating something, and when I say something I mean steak, ribs, a hamburger, like anyone else, but I was in Romania, comrades, and by that time the *Conducatore* had already decided to export all agricultural produce, condemning those of us who lived in the socialist paradise to eat *bazofia*, a sausage made from tripe and offal. It smelled and tasted like shit, but even so I couldn't get them to sell me a few slices, because my ration card—the titan of titans made sure everyone was happy and equal by issuing ration cards—could only be used in my own neighborhood.

"I went back to where I was living, the residential collective for persecuted comrades from Asia, Africa and Latin America, and there was Constantinescu, furious because I hadn't waited for him when I left the theater. Then I lifted my hand to my head for the second time, and once again Constantinescu put my hair in a little bag. To my astonishment, the following morning he left me alone. I realized I had to ration all this tearing out of hair, and at the same time started preparing my escape.

"For years I've had one obsession: to go back to Bucharest and look for my file in the Securitate archives. What the hell did they do with my hair? Anyway, one day, when I was already nearly as bald as you see me now, I took advantage of Comrade Constantinescu's absence, walked to the railroad track, and climbed on a train loaded with beetroot and heading in a westerly direction. I slept among the beetroot, and when I woke up I was in Yugoslavia. Some militiamen took me down from the train. I didn't speak a single word of Serbian, but they realized I wasn't Romanian, and, after repeating the word Chile several times, I ended up bawling at the top of my voice while I stuffed myself with *sarma*, an incredible kind of paella that uses every possible part of the pig, and the glasses of slivovitz those Yugoslav militiamen generously plied me with made me the happiest bald man on earth."

"You were in the land of Marshal Tito," Arancibia said, "the one anti-Fascist partisan who ended up as a head of state. I hope you felt proud."

"I felt hungry and western," Garmendia replied. "And anyway, my dear Lucho, there was another partisan who ended up as a head of state: Willy Brandt, but he didn't make such a fuss about it. Better pass me a chicken thigh." The three men moved closer to the plasterboard table, and even Salinas took a breast. These chickens didn't taste so bad, the condiments had magically reduced their insipid quality.

They ate, drank, and talked of their lives, while the rain, which showed no sign of stopping, clattered on the roof. They didn't say so, but the three of them felt good here, by the fire. They talked, reviving the lost national custom of a good chat over wine, and looked at each other without any suspicion, because whether they were fatter or thinner, bald or with a graying beard, they knew for sure there are still tigers who don't care whether they have one stripe more or one stripe less. Even Lucho Arancibia's story—his two brothers swallowed up by the darkness of the dictatorship, his experiences in the military prison on Calle de Londres and later the concentration camp at Puchuncaví, from which he emerged, as he himself said, with his head messed up—was just another conversation between Chileans, between South Americans, between inhabitants of the same fucked-up southern part of the world.

"Lolo," Salinas said, "who the hell are we waiting for?"

"The specialist," Arancibia said. "I already told you."

"What's going on, Lolo?" Salinas insisted.

"It's very simple," Garmendia replied. "We're going to rob a bank."

The three men sat there in silence, staring into the fire.

9.

Concepción García poured herself a fifth glass of *aguardiente* and stammered something about going out on the balcony, because their apartment on Jakobstrasse had had one, and in that small space adorned with flowerpots she used to read the *Tageszeitung* to decide what concert, movie or exhibition she would go to the following day.

Her husband looked at her, perplexed. "What balcony? Concha, we aren't in Berlin anymore, we're in Santiago and we don't have a balcony here. What you have to do is keep calm and listen to what I'm saying."

Aravena continued explaining to her that the police always come in twos, so that they can play the good cop bad cop game. That meant they would arrive as a pair and would insist on questioning them separately. That was where that short skirt she still had would come into play, with no panties or anything else underneath. Obviously, she wasn't Sharon Stone, but none of the police officers would be Michael Douglas either, so that even here the trick of slowly crossing her legs would arouse the cops' *basic instinct*. Everything depended on her powers of seduction.

Aravena broke off his lesson on witness behavior and looked at the thin thread of saliva coming out of his wife's mouth. She had fallen asleep on the couch.

"Concha," Aravena muttered, "you knocked back half a bottle of *aguardiente*." He shook her, and realized that the only way she could sober up was by sleeping it off. It was all in his hands now. He had to prepare a convincing story, a cast-iron alibi.

"It was like this, officer. I left the building to go to the video store. I was planning to rent *Paint Your Wagon*, because I'm a great fan of classic westerns and Lee Marvin has a big part in that movie. Suddenly I saw a car pull up, a huge black Chrysler with the windows tinted so that I couldn't see who was inside. They fired at this man on the street and drove off. I was torn between following the vehicle and helping the man, who had a wound in his head and was losing blood, but it was already too late to do anything. No, I couldn't see the license number, as you can imagine, it's not possible to see anything in all this rain . . ."

No, Coco, they won't swallow that. You're describing the kind of vehicle the FBI or the yakuza might use. It's not the kind of thing you find much in Chile, Coco, so your whole idea is a tall story, what we call a *goat*.

A goat, that's what it is. A goat is just a quadruped, anywhere in the world except in Chile. In Scandinavia or Australia, a goat is a stubborn animal, impervious to argument. That's how it is on any New Zealand farm, Asturian meadow, Caribbean island, but not in Chile, because in this long strip of land that, seen through the lens of Google Earth, looks like a remnant of the continent, a leftover piece that'll soon be trimmed and snipped by the great tailor of the sea, a goat is the ultimate proof of sly ingenuity, it sums up all that terrible Spanish guile, the worst of inheritances. A goat is a convincing, well-constructed lie, better than the reality it replaces. That's the way it is, Coco.

"The truth of the matter, officer, is that I left home with two ideas in my mind. The first was to buy a carton of red wine to make mulled wine, you can't go wrong on a rainy night with a mulled wine with oranges and cinnamon, of course it has to be cheap wine, you don't pour a bottle of Concha y Toro into a pot. The second idea was to go to the video store and see if they had the Japanese classic *The Seven Samurai*. I love Toshiro Mifune in the role of that half-naked samurai who the other six don't take seriously. I was just trying to make up my mind whether I should go first to the liquor store or the video store, when suddenly this man grabs me, and asks for help, and just then I realize that two very tall, well-built guys with fair hair and masks are charging at me and making threatening gestures. That's right, they had masks on, Halloween masks, you know what I mean, smiling pumpkins, things like that. It all happened very quickly. I practice tae kwon do, so I got into a simultaneous attack and defense position, but I couldn't stop one of the Slavs, yes, they were Slavs, they called each other *tovarich*, hitting the poor man with the handle of a gun. It was a Glock, no doubt about that, those Austrian guns are unmistakable. When I saw the man go down, I assumed a more aggressive attack position, and the guys realized they were dealing with an opponent who was experienced in martial arts and ran off toward a vehicle that was waiting for them a short distance away with its doors open. It was a Land Rover and its license plates were covered in mud. The poor man. Before dying, he looked me in the eyes and said this was the beginning of a beautiful friendship. I'm still in shock…"

No, Coco, they definitely won't swallow that. Forget *Casablanca* and tae kwon do. The guy just died, without saying a word. Get a grip, Coco.

"It all happened very quickly, officer, so there may well be a few gaps in my testimony, or pieces that don't fit, as you so nicely put it in your professional jargon. But, keeping strictly to the facts, this is more or less what happened: I was closing the street door, double-locking it, because there have been quite a few burglaries in the area lately. I was going to the video store, intending to rent *Titanic*, not that I'm especially fond of Leonardo DiCaprio, no, I don't find him very convincing with that face of his like a little boy who still pisses his pants. What I like about that movie is the love story, the poor artist and the rich girl who falls madly in love with him. When you get down to it, it's one more version of the old Shakespeare play, but what are the classics of the giant screen but new versions of old dramas? That's a digression, I know, but it's illustrative of my state of mind when the tragedy took place. I was putting my key ring in my pocket when a luxury car, a sinister-looking black Mercedes, stopped a few yards from where I was. Immediately, the door opened and the poor man fell out onto the sidewalk. Clearly he was scared and was trying to run away. He muttered a few words that I couldn't hear because of the noise of the rain, maybe a tragic cry for help, and then only a few seconds later, a tall, heavy-set man got out of the car. He was black, possibly an African from Kenya, unmistakable, really, because you don't see many Africans in this neighborhood. Because of the rain, his black skin was glistening in the most terrifying way, yes, I admit I was scared, I'm a peace-loving man. The African, who, now that I think of it, might not have been a Kenyan but a Zulu, strode toward the other poor devil. When he got to him, I saw he was carrying a briefcase, one of those typical executive briefcases used by Mafiosi to carry bribes or ransom money. I'm not sure, but I think I yelled at him to leave the other man alone, but the black man thrust me unceremoniously aside. To be honest, he gave me a tremendous shove that almost made me lose my balance, and then, taking advantage of my confusion, hit the poor man hard with his briefcase, and the victim of the attack collapsed on the spot. The impact made the briefcase fly open, and three heavy objects fell out. I immediately recognized them: three gold ingots with a swastika clearly embossed on them. I reacted with the indignation that any sensible man would feel and gave the black man a couple of kicks as he was picking up the ingots, and I suppose I must have done him some damage, since he limped to the car howling wildly with pain . . ."

No, Coco, come on, you must be joking.

Coco Aravena scratched his head, cursed his screen-writer's imagination, looked at his wife, who was still asleep, and walked into the bedroom. There, he lifted the mattress and took out the heavy revolver.

"Let's look at things calmly," he muttered in a low voice, with the weapon in his hands. "No one actually saw what happened. Sooner or later they'll catch the thieves who stole the shoes. They'll beat them up in the cellar and pin the death on them. The guy wasn't a cop. Cops carry badges, a cop without a badge is naked, worse than that, he's like a eunuch. So what do we have? A man with a gun and no ID. A gangster? It doesn't make sense, a gangster wouldn't go out alone without spare ammunition. A hit-man? That can't be right either. Hitmen go around in inconspicuous cars, never on foot. What are we left with? The dirty side of politics. The dead man was working for a secret service, maybe he was an Argentine, Bolivian, or Peruvian spy, there's no shortage of countries that have old quarrels with Chile. And apart from that, there's this telephone number."

Coco Aravena picked up the phone from the bedside table, dialed, and waited, covering his mouth with his free hand.

"We're ready," a man's voice said.

"Good," Aravena replied.

"Write down the address," the voice said.

Coco Aravena wrote it on the palm of his hand.

"Oh, and over the door there's a sign that says *Arancibia Garage*," the voice said.

Before he hung up, Aravena heard another man say, "Ask him if he likes chicken."

10

Concepción García's mouth was dry, her palate half numbed by the *aguardiente*. She was dying for a big glass of *Schorle*, that happy mixture of beer and lemonade, perfect for curing hangovers.

The aroma of freshly brewed coffee revived her a little, and she realized, as if for the first time, that the girl in the dark blue vest with the words CRIMINAL INVESTIGATIONS on the back was real, and so was the man sitting at the other end of the table looking at her with an amused expression.

"How are you feeling, señora?" the man asked.

The woman took a sip of coffee and asked about her husband.

"We don't know where he is. We called, you opened the door, offered us a drink, and then dropped like a sack of potatoes, if you'll pardon the expression. Detective Bobadilla here managed to revive you. I'm Inspector Manuel Crespo and I need to ask you a few questions."

The woman remembered something her husband had said about good cops and bad cops.

"Go ahead."

"A couple of hours ago, you and your husband went to your local police station and reported that some electrical appliances had been stolen. What did the thieves take?"

"My husband knows, he made the list."

"And unfortunately you don't know your husband's whereabouts. Señora, at a glance I can see an electric coffee maker, a toaster, a microwave, a TV set, and a video recorder, which are the things thieves usually take. I repeat: what did they steal?"

"*Scheisse*," the woman murmured.

"German for shit," the inspector noted. "No, señora, thieves don't usually steal shit."

The woman leaned her elbows on the table and put her head in her hands. She closed her eyes tightly, the trick had to work for once and help her disappear. She felt the girl's hand on her shoulder, and moved it gently away, without pressing.

"What happened on the street?" the girl asked.

Concepción García opened her eyes, looked at the dark surface of the coffee, and saw herself on a march together with thousands of people chanting slogans bursting with confidence, saw the red flags of the Communist party, the red flags of the Socialists, the red and black flags of the Left Revolutionary Movement and, farther back, almost at the end of the procession, a young man carrying a huge banner with the image of a fat, smiling man who was unfamiliar to her. She saw herself going up to him and heard herself asking innocently who the fat man was. "That's Chairman Mao, the Great Helmsman," the young man had replied, and had then introduced himself as Jorge, Coco to his girlfriends, and invited her to have a refreshing maize and peach drink after the demonstration. She saw herself captivated by this guy who was against everything and for whom those hundred thousand people on the march were nothing more than misguided puppets of Soviet social imperialism, basically petit bourgeois or lumpenproletariat counter-revolutionaries. A guy capable of coming out with such unexpected insults was indeed captivating and, for a young female worker in the Vestex textile factory, a really amusing person.

On the dark screen of the coffee, life passed swiftly, their brief romance, their marriage, her family's disappointment at her marrying a short guy who refused a Catholic wedding, arguing that religion was the opium of the people, and who converted the ceremony, which, as a civil rite, was already pretty austere, into a kind of Amish festival or a convention of elevator operators, because his groomsmen were all dressed exactly alike, in jackets buttoned up to the neck and red copies of *On the Correct Handling of Contradictions Among the People* stuck to their chests like nipples. Next came her hopes that one day Coco would stop being a fanatic, especially when he responded to suggestions that he should look for a job by brandishing a little red book in a plastic cover that from a distance looked like a first communion booklet, although the title said it was *Five Theses Against Liberalism*. Across the surface of the coffee, she saw her workmates at the textile factory pass, one after the other, all relentless in their arguments, such as "Where did you pick up that fucking Chinaman?" or "Political activist my eye, he's a shirker, that's what he is," or "If I were in your place I'd have given him a kick in the ass a long time ago."

The coffee thickened in the cup as the images of the coup gave way to Coco Aravena resolutely justifying the Chinese government, which had locked and barred the doors of its embassy to prevent any Chilean from finding asylum within the walls of the Great Helmsman's house.

Across the cup passed dead bodies floating in the thick dark waters of the river Mapocho, bodies of union leaders from the textile factory left at the gates of the factory itself, riddled with bullets, during curfew, and finally the toothless face of a neighbor telling her to run to her house because her husband was on the phone. "I'm in the German embassy, I can't stand the repression" was all he said, to which she replied, "For God's sake, Coco, no one's after you." And finally she had a distinct image of her faraway apartment in Kreuzberg, in a Berlin that was now lost forever.

"I killed him," Concepción García said.

Detective Adela Bobadilla and Inspector Crespo looked at each other. They both knew that confessing to a crime they hadn't even been asking about lacked credibility, especially coming from a woman who'd just been awakened from a drunken stupor.

"Drink your coffee, señora," Detective Bobadilla said. "I can warm it up for you if you like."

But the woman pushed the cup away. "No, let's get this over with first. I killed him. Handcuff me."

"Let's take things one at a time, señora," the inspector said. "Who the hell did you kill?"

Then Concepción García gave quite a coherent, detailed description of a life full of doubts and frustration, with few expectations and an indolent husband who—or so the two police officers gathered—had moved in the 1980s from political radicalism to a life devoted to the seventh art, at least as a home viewer.

As she went on with her account, the woman calmed down. She took them into the living room so they could see the broken window panes, covered by a blanket that was already starting to drip, and then the cabinet from which she had taken the objects she had thrown into the street.

"I know it's too late now, but it was unintentional. I've never harmed a fly and now I'm a murderer." That was the last thing she said.

"I could really use a coffee," the inspector suggested. He would have liked to talk about the rain, because that was what you did when it rained, you talked about how in the old days it really rained, do you remember the storms of '62? Instead of which, he threw in two spoonfuls of sugar, stirred them slowly, and thought about how easy it is to cross the line between life and death. He remembered an accident, apparently caused by negligence, that had cost the lives of two people. A driver turned left on a street and ran straight into a van coming, according to him, from the opposite direction. The impact wasn't great, and yet it was strong enough for a spark to hit the gas tank, which was covered with nothing but a cloth. The explosion and the ensuing fire killed the two occupants of the van. The driver of the car that caused the tragedy escaped, but gave himself up to the police a few hours later.

He was another man who had just returned from exile, after fifteen years in Prague, and in his defense he claimed that the accident had taken place in his own neighborhood, that his whole life traffic on that street had gone from north to south, and that he did not know when it had changed direction. People returning from exile were often disoriented, the city wasn't the same, they looked for their usual bars and found Chinese stores, their childhood pharmacy was now a topless joint, their old school a car showroom, the local movie house a Pentecostal temple. Without warning, their country had changed.

"You aren't a murderer," the inspector said. "It was an accident. You were careless, of course, although, if you've told us the whole truth, and we think you have, you were blinded by anger."

"But you are going to arrest me, aren't you?" the woman asked.

"No. What would be the point of that? Besides, it's still raining cats and dogs. Stay here, keep calm, and at eight o'clock tomorrow morning come down to headquarters. Bring a change of underwear, some toiletries, and a couple of books, because we're going to detain you, possibly charging you with causing death by criminal negligence. You'll have to stay in custody for a few days until the judge fixes bail. And now we need to talk to your husband."

Concepción García did not know her husband's whereabouts. She told them about the two places he went to most often, the video store, and the Internet café in the shopping mall, which would both be closed at this hour of the night.

The police officers made as if to take their leave, and at that moment she saw herself standing at the broken window while her husband examined the dead man. She went back to the bedroom and lifted the mattress.

"There's something I didn't tell you. He had a gun, my husband put it here, but it's not here now."

Detective Bobadilla remembered the first day she had worked with Inspector Crespo. Among the general remarks he made, he mentioned that he liked to take things calmly. That was his only method, the only way not to be overwhelmed by imponderables. And there was never an investigation that didn't have imponderables.

"Señora," he asked, "do you have a telephone in the house?"

The woman nodded and Adelita wrote down her cell phone number for her.

Before starting the car, she waited for the inspector to calm down. It was still raining hard over Santiago, flashes of lightning lit up the darkness and the rolling thunder made the street lamps quiver.

"The first question is: What was Pedrito doing with that gun? The second is: What's our missing husband doing with it now? I once read a brilliant mystery novel by Chester Himes called *Blind Man with a Pistol*, and liked it so much, I read it several times. Let's hope our armed husband doesn't go any further than that."

"What's our next step?" Detective Bobadilla asked.

"Let's be on the alert for men who look married."

11

Message from gerund@hotmail.com
to blackpanther@hotmail.com
I'm pleased to hear from you, I came back less than six months ago and as you see I got a hotmail account that I mustn't give to anybody. It's all right, I don't have any friends left. What's this all about? It all seems very mysterious. And please don't write to me using that illiterate grammar the young use. I want complete words, not u for you and that kind of thing.

Message from blackpanther@hotmail.com
to gerund@hotmail.com
I'm also pleased to know you're alive. My list of friends has a lot of crosses on it. Tell me how you are: a) your love life; b) your financial situation; and c) do you think you'll stay in the country? Whether I finally tell you what this is all about will depend on your answers. In the same order, my own answers are: a) I married a Croatian woman in '86, the marriage lasted one child and four years, now I'm divorced and looking for a girlfriend on the Internet; b) fucked, even though I inherited my parents' house and don't have to pay rent. I'm unemployed, and when you're a senior that isn't a good situation to be in; c) I feel as if I'm just passing through and want to go back to Europe.

Message from gerund@hotmail.com
to blackpanther@hotmail.com
a) Similar situation, though my wife wasn't Croatian, I married my old sweetheart, Matilde, we had a son who made me a grandfather, and she discovered French love. From the point of view of pure reason, emotionally I'm like the planks of a henhouse: covered in shit. Tell me what it's like, looking for a girlfriend on the Internet; b) I'm a journalist, or rather I was, it's been quite a while since I last wrote a line. I live in a fairly decent boarding house, and every day I go out to look for something without knowing what the hell it is I'm looking for, which makes it unlikely I'll find it; c) I hadn't thought about it, although I think I'd be happy to go north and live like an ageing hippie in San Pedro de Atacama. I hate Santiago.

Message from blackpanther@hotmail.com
to gerund@hotmail.com
Satisfactory replies. I remember Matilde, at university she was pretty enough to eat, and when you talk about French love do you mean she left you for a frog? Was the honor of the fatherland besmirched? It was a Bosnian who fucked things up for me. I'll explain: people stopped being moved by the tragedy of the Chileans when the dictatorship ended, and once the war in the Balkans had started it was the Bosnians who became the mambo kings. About looking for a girlfriend on the Internet, it's quite simple. There are sites like glassslipper.com. Look on the web, register, write an ad, putting something like "mature romantic seeks partner," indicate your preferences, and wait. You can also cut things short by looking in the small ads. Do you know how to chat? Two pieces of advice: don't believe everything

you see, the photographs are often of other girls who are twenty years younger and quite different in height and weight than the real advertisers. The other piece of advice is: invent a decent nickname, there are guys who call themselves tenjuicyinches or itsaboysaidthemidwife, and I'm sure they get absolutely nowhere. Last question: what do you think of Robin Hood?

Message from gerund@hotmail.com
to blackpanther@hotmail.com
Your message is a bit vague. I'm genuinely sorry about the Bosnian. I don't know if you remember that Matilde was a cultured woman. Her French love has a vineyard in Provence and an apartment on the Rive Gauche in Paris, and he's a literary critic. No comment. I followed your instructions and went on the glass slipper website. My nickname is chubbyromantic, and I cut things short. I'm chatting with someone called lonelysoul and things are looking promising. She can make tamales and maize cakes and once won the Miss Mondongo contest. I don't know what I think about Robin Hood, he was English and history tells me that most Englishman aren't so noble. If he robbed the rich to give to the poor I'll endorse his cause, but I think they told us the story all wrong and the guy's name was Hobin Rood and he robbed the poor to give to the rich, which is a very Anglo-Saxon custom. Why all the mystery? One last thing: Miss Mondongo has suggested we send each other photographs. Tell me what I should do.

Message from blackpanther@hotmail.com
to gerund@hotmail.com
Robin Hood: Once upon a time there was a Chilean ban-

dit who robbed the rich, but although he was well inten-
tioned, he didn't have time to divide up the booty among
the poor. He put it in Ali Baba's cave, and then he died.
I know where the cave is and we are poor. We equals
three: you, me and do you remember the delegate for
paste? I like this Miss Mondongo. For the photos you
have to go to a photographer, let him do you a couple of
good photos and give them to you on a CD. Then you put
them in the computer and send them. Careful, if she asks
you for a roll of film you would have to get hold of a dig-
ital camera and take them yourself. Question: would you
go to Ali Baba's cave?

Message from gerund@hotmail.com
to blackpanther@hotmail.com
Do you send rolls of film? Miss Mondongo wants pass-
port-size photos and we already agree on a number of
things: we both like eating well and drinking in modera-
tion. At least it's a step. What you're suggesting sounds
serious. Let's have a drink at Las Tejas, if the place still
exists, and we can talk face to face. The delegate for
paste: was that the guy who had a garage? He made the
best paste in the world, without lumps, creamy and light.
He really made you want to go out and put up posters
when he made paste. Let's meet tomorrow at noon.

Message from Blackpanther@hotmail.com
to gerund@hotmail.com
Negative. When we made contact I told you we couldn't
meet until we clarified certain details. Robin Hood was
the detail. As Herminio Iglesias, the great Argentine
union leader, said, I'll do it with me or without me, and

the fewer faces you know, the better. Robin Hood's treasure is the color of a fat frog. It's all hush-hush and ultra safe. In addition, we can count on the collaboration of a specialist. The delegate for paste also remembers you. He had a bad time but is still working hard. He asks, Are you in? If you decide not to do it, simply don't answer this message. Good luck with Miss Mondongo.

Message from gerund@hotmail.com
to blackpanther@hotmail.com
You mentioned a specialist. Does that mean that the frog has four feet? I accept. There is nothing worse than the thing we plan but don't do. Miss Mondongo knows a bit about astrology, she did my chart and says—and I quote —that she sees me in the company of three gentlemen sharing a moment of glory. When?

Message from blackpanther@hotmail.com
to gerund@hotmail.com
I was sure I could count on you. The specialist is doing it for romantic reasons, and the frog has three legs. I like your Miss Mondongo better every day. Do you remember the address of the garage? The date is tomorrow. Get here between eight and ten in the evening. I'm putting you in charge of the food. You may find the delegate for paste a bit eccentric. Those bastards messed with his head, but I regard him as my left testicle and he is offering us his garage. Has Miss Mondongo sent you any photographs?

Message from gerund@hotmail.com
to blackpanther@hotmail.com
I'll be there. What shall I buy? Miss Mondongo sent me

three photographs of herself in her bikini. Long live big girls. What you said about his head being messed up, is it serious? I'm getting excited: Miss Mondongo sees me close to the stars and San Pedro de Atacama has the biggest astronomical observatories. If the frog is fat, I see myself with her (Miss Mondongo, not the frog) every day in the sun in the valley of the moon.

Message from blackpanther@hotmail.com
to gerund@hotmail.com
The thing about his head isn't serious. He's waiting for you. If he starts to get weird, just go with the flow. Ask Miss Mondongo if she has a sister or friend like her. This is our last message. Buy chickens. Just around the corner from the garage there's a place that sells chickens 24 hours a day.

12.

Coco Aravena was sorry he hadn't taken his umbrella when he left home. The rain was unusually heavy and it was quite cold. When day broke, if it cleared up, the snowcapped Andes would look radiant. Santiago would be the city hemmed in by symbols of winter that Silvio Rodríguez had sung about.

He walked quickly past the front door, saw the old sign saying *Arancibia Garage*. He could feel the revolver in the pocket weighing down his soaking overcoat. He reached the corner and sheltered from the rain in a doorway. He lit a cigarette and set his brain to work.

The likeliest thing is that they're from the Bolivian secret service. What are they called? The Yanks call the CIA the Company. What shall I tell them? It probably wasn't such a brilliant idea to call them, if they're good they'll already have traced my phone, these people have scanners and sensors. The truth. My truth anyway: I witnessed their man's death, and if it's of any help I can assure them that he withstood torture without giving anything away. He asked me to give them back their gun, yes, he and I had met on other missions which for security reasons you are not supposed to know about. There's no point going so close to the edge that you get dizzy . . .

No, Coco, you're starting with your stories again.

Shit, this gun's heavy. Come to think of it, it's an old gun, and it's unlikely that secret service agents would carry obsolete weapons. There's nothing sophisticated about a gun like this, it takes too long to reload. No, they aren't Bolivian spies. What an idiot I am! That guy was from the Office. The garage must be the headquarters of the Office. That's why he was carrying an old revolver. Kill, then throw it away. That's it. No one can keep a secret in this country, there's not enough space, and everyone knows that back during the first democratic government they decided to create an unofficial security body, the Office, to kill the last leftists who still thought it possible to defeat the dictatorship by force of arms. They invented an excuse even they didn't believe: to create a dialogue from a position on the left, especially with the Manuel Rodríguez Patriotic Front, who were a thorn in Pinochet's side, all the while knowing they were going to liquidate anyone who wouldn't accept their point of view, anyone who didn't understand that Chile's transition to democracy was made according to the maxim from *The Leopard* that everything changes so that everything can remain the same. When they were still in exile, some members of the Office formed partnerships with torturers and started security companies. Now they're rich, they own private police forces that guard banks and office blocks and those exclusive gated communities in the Andean valleys where you can breathe fresh air while Santiago is choked with smog. The Office. It can't be anything else. Yes, your man always trusted me, I was his shadow on a lot of missions, his unknown helper, the infrastructure that must have surprised you more than once. He's been given a major job, boys, so don't feel bad. All I can tell you is that right now he's on a plane to Namibia, and it's something to do with diamonds. He asked me to give you this back and pass on to you his final message, which is that there's no point trying to get in contact with him.

Not bad, Coco. Not bad at all.

Another flash of lightning lit up the street, and rain lashed the sidewalks. Coco Aravena came to a halt in front of the door and rapped on it with his knuckles. He assumed the door would be opened by a silent man wearing a mask, who would probably blindfold him before taking him to the men in charge of the Office, instead of which there was Lucho Arancibia looking at him with his eyes popping out of his head and then grabbing him by the lapels.

Coco Aravena next saw Lolo Garmendia, bald now but still recognizable despite the thirty-something years since he had last seen him. Next to him was Cacho Salinas, fatter, with a white beard and an astonished expression, although not as astonished as the one on the face of the man who had opened the door to him and had still not let go of his lapels.

"Are you the Office?" he stammered, gripped firmly by Arancibia.

"What about you?" Garmendia asked, lifting his hands to his bald head. "Who asked you to butt in here?"

:

13.

Inspector Crespo tuned to Radio Cooperativa just as the weather forecast was predicting that the rain would continue for another forty-eight hours. The metropolitan region was on the alert for floods, there was a warning not to go too close to the banks of the canals, and it was announced that all schools would be closed the following day.

"At least someone's benefiting from this," he murmured.

"We've been driving around for more than an hour, inspector," Detective Bobadilla said. "Aren't you hungry?"

Since they had left Concepción García, they had done nothing but cruise around at less than twenty miles an hour. The empty streets awash with rain and the welcoming warmth of the patrol car were conducive to drowsiness, but they were still alert. They had stopped three different men in a hurry. One was immediately ruled out, because, according to the inspector, he had the face of a single man—a distinction Detective Bobadilla found hard to grasp—and the others gave satisfactory answers.

"Go south along Santa Rosa. Do you know the Chancho Monono?"

It was midnight by the time they entered the old restaurant on the Gran Avenida. A few customers sat at one of the tables, watching TV on a set some distance from them.

"Inspector Crespo, what an honor!" the owner said by way of greeting.

"Give us two legs of pork with mashed potatoes, plenty of chili, and some German mustard," the inspector ordered.

"And tea," Detective Bobadilla added. "Make sure it's nice and hot."

The inspector was scratching his two-day beard, a gesture he often made when he was thinking. "I don't like it that this guy's walking around armed. I certainly don't like it that Pedro went out with a gun. What was he up to? Where was he going?"

"I get the impression you knew him well," Detective Bobadilla said. "I think you liked him."

"He was a lone wolf, Adelita, an outsider. His parents died in an accident when he was two years old and he was brought up by his grandfather, an anarchist, the very same one who robbed the Bank of Chile in 1925 with Buenaventura Durruti, Gregorio Jover and Francisco Ascaso. His grandfather instilled in him the strict morality of the anarchists and gave him lessons in going underground that no one in Chile had ever had. Eat, these legs of pork are from recently weaned piglets, and I'll tell you how I met him."

Detective Bobadilla cut herself a piece of pork, smeared it with mustard, and raised it to her mouth. The meat was tender and tasty, and fragrant with the celery and bay leaves used in the cooking.

"In 1969, I left the police academy and started working in the Criminal Investigations Department. In May of the following year, the Marines attacked a supposed guerilla training camp in the south, in the Mapuche region. The place was called Chaihuín, a godforsaken spot in the mountains, always cold and snowy, with rivers flowing down to the Pacific. It had nothing to do with the Marines, it was a political matter, we were living in a democracy, the police were accountable to the Ministry of the Interior, but the Marines painted their faces and attacked.

"It was just a bunch of Young Socialists, most of them university students, who were training in the use of arms and guerilla techniques. There was a shootout, and everything could have ended with the apprentice guerrillas' surrender, but that wasn't what happened because the Marines had specific orders to go after one person, who had to disappear. His name was Kiko Barraza, he'd been a cadet in the naval academy, with a brilliant future ahead of him, instead of which he'd deserted and joined these hypothetical guerrillas. Yes, Adelita, he was a deserter, and the Chilean naval academy, with its ridiculous English rules of discipline, doesn't forgive deserters. And it wasn't just a question of desertion. It was mostly the sons of the very rich who went to the naval academy, members of the elite, destined to sail the seven seas on *La Esmeralda*, their endless tours of duty paid for from the public purse. It was very rare that anyone middle-class got in, especially if they didn't have naval ancestors and weren't blond and blue-eyed. Somehow, Kiko Barraza gained admission to the naval academy and distinguished himself as a seaman. Because of his appearance, he was nicknamed the Indian, but he didn't care. He was strong, more than six feet tall, was always the first to climb the mast, and knew the sea like the back of his hand. In addition, he was a poet, the worst affront to the masculinity of those Creole Nelsons. So they made sure he disappeared. No one ever saw him again. And since there were only four months to the presidential election, the case was closed without any investigation into what had happened.

"Two weeks after the attack on Chaihuín, by which time people had stopped talking about it because the election was getting everyone's attention—it looked very likely that Allende would win, and the right, as well as being in a state of hysteria, seemed to be divided—one day, as I left headquarters, a man came up to me and said, 'Hey, Johnny Law, I want to talk to you.'

"I'll never forget it, because that encounter almost made me quit the police. I'm an avid reader of detective novels, Adelita, and in those novels justice always triumphs, and if the law has to be bent a little it's precisely so that justice will triumph. I pretended to ignore the fact that he called me Johnny Law, these days no officer would be bothered if he was called that, and I asked him what he wanted. He wanted to know who was in charge of the investigation into the disappearance of Kiko Barraza and I told him no one, as there'd been orders from higher up to close the case.

"'They took him alive and killed him,' he said, looking me straight in the eye. I asked him how he knew and his reply was disconcertingly straight: 'Because I was with him and I saw the whole thing. I have proof, witnesses, I can identify the officers who killed him. Well, Johnny, are you in?'

"I was an ordinary, inexperienced detective, and I told him so.

"'In other words you can't do anything. Listen, Johnny, I don't think you believe me. Never mind, we're going to recover the weapons Kiko's murderers took and we'll do it in a spectacular fashion. If you're thinking of arresting me right now, Johnny, you're wasting your time. I don't leave traces, and you have no witnesses to this conversation. And another thing, Johnny, the Chaihuín boys wanted to learn how to fight in order to be free, and that's what all these people betting on Allende are doing, too. They want to be free. I'm different, Johnny. I'm fighting so as not to forget I'm already free.'

"As you can imagine, Adelita, I didn't tell any of my superiors about my conversation with Pedrito. I kept asking myself why he had chosen me and never came up with an answer.

"A week later, the alarms went off at eight in the morning. There had been a spectacular robbery at the Italian Armory. We went there armed, wearing bulletproof vests, and with helicopter support, because no one knew if the thieves were still inside the armory. In the jargon of the left, it was known as Operation Wonderful. The robbery was committed by a commando called Pedro Lenín Valenzuela, after a young boy who two years earlier had tried to hijack a Lan Chile plane, on the ground, to take him to Cuba. The boy had died on the plane, riddled with bullets. No one had ever intended to negotiate, we've always had a lot of psychopaths with itchy trigger fingers.

"We entered the armory. The only thing we found was a note from the commandos, saying they had recovered the weapons taken from Chaihuín and demanding justice for Kiko Barraza. And we also found dozens of witnesses and what they told us made the robbery seem even more spectacular.

"Two members of the commando unit had stayed in a boarding house next to the armory. They had gathered all the guests in one room, and opened the door to let other members in. They split into two groups, one to make a hole in the wall and get into the armory and the others to keep an eye on the guests. Everyone agreed they were young, polite, friendly, and hadn't been violent in any way. Among the guests there was a couple with a baby who wouldn't stop crying. This drew the attention of one of the commandos, who said he was a medical student and asked permission to examine the baby. He diagnosed bronchitis, and asked where the parents were from. It turned out they were from Lota and the baby had breathed in too much coal dust. Through a walkie-talkie, they asked for someone on the outside to go to an emergency pharmacy with the prescription the medical student wrote out. For some strange reason, the walkie-talkies were tuned to the same frequency as the police radios, so some of my colleagues listened in to the instructions on how to make a bottle for the baby. About twenty people took part in the robbery, maybe more, no one ever knew for sure. From the little we were able to find out, we know, for example, that one of our most famous writers was helping them on the outside, keeping a look out while putting up posters for Odontine toothpaste on the walls near the armory.

"The Italian armory raid was really spectacular, Adelita, and we were left looking like complete idiots. It was never established how many weapons were taken, or what they were, because the people in charge refused to release a list or give any information about where the weapons came from.

"Two or three days after the robbery I saw Pedrito again. He was waiting for me opposite headquarters, sitting on the steps of the prison. He waved at me as I came out.

"'Well, Johnny, are you in or not?'

"I didn't know what to say. I could have overpowered him, handcuffed him, taken him down into the cellars, where a dumb former heavyweight champion named Arturo Godoy worked, beating confessions out of prisoners. But the man didn't leave tracks, Adelita. He was like a shadow.

"I didn't do anything, except think about how I liked being a policeman.

"'Never mind, Johnny. I just want to ask you to think about this: the boys don't want violence, but they're ready to respond. Be decent. Ciao, Johnny.'

"I suppose I paid attention to what he said, because I'm retiring this year with a shit pension, like all decent police officers. Don't let me talk too long, Adelita. Can't you see my leg of pork has gotten cold?"

"Ask for another one. I like listening to you, because you think before you speak. Well, inspector?"

"It doesn't make sense that he'd be carrying a gun, Pedrito was never violent. And we don't know much about this armed husband."

14

Coco Aravena was looking at the three men as they smoked in silence, sipped their wine and moved their heads glumly. Several minutes passed in this way. The only kindness they showed him consisted of Arancibia letting go of him and pushing him toward the plasterboard table.

"I'm getting out of here," Cacho Salinas said.

"Wait," Garmendia interrupted. "Do you think I knew this idiot was going to show up?"

"Could I have some wine?" Coco Aravena asked.

"Top or bottom?" Lucho Arancibia said, and the other two burst out laughing. Even Aravena smiled, although with a certain lack of conviction.

Then he recognized him. How he had changed, how old he looked, that old *tonton macoute* of the Ramona Parra Brigade, the Young Communist shock troops, the man responsible for the biggest humiliation he had ever suffered during his life as a militant.

It was in 1971. Socialists and Communists had summoned a meeting in the Pedagogical Institute to inform people about the popular government's literacy campaign and to ask for volunteers, as well as telling them about the challenges facing the production sector.

There was a great deal of enthusiasm in the hall; people asked to speak, and identified themselves: "So and so, from the committee of the philosophy faculty. We have comrades ready to go out into the fields and take part in the literacy campaign provided we can solve the problem of transportation." "So and so, from the journalism committee: Comrades, we seem to be neglecting the task of bringing literacy to the mines. Let's not forget that the miners are the vanguard of the working class." Commissions were appointed, couples formed, people sang with their fists in the air.

There in the middle of the assembly, Coco Aravena felt euphoric. The commission for agitation and propaganda of the Marxist-Leninist Communist Revolutionary Party, Mao Tse-Tung Thought, Enver Hoxha Tendency, which was very different than the liquidationist clique that called itself the Marxist-Leninist Communist Revolutionary Party, Mao Tse-Tung Thought, Red Flag Tendency, had commissioned him to read a resolution from the central committee, a resolution destined to change history.

He was given permission to speak, and started reading out a pamphlet that criticized the conduct of the war in Vietnam with unusual harshness, accusing the Vietcong and Ho Chi Minh of social imperialist deviationism, but was unable to continue because Arancibia, who was wearing the armband of the Ramona Parra Brigade, grabbed hold of him with his strong hands and led him to the far end of the hall. There, he was surrounded by a dozen brigade members who, as well as making comments on the nerve of these fucking pro-Chinese, were eyeing him with obvious hostility.

Coco Aravena tried to hand out a few pamphlets to the brigade members, the great truths of the Party were in them, but none of them took their hands out of their pockets.

"Let's see, Chinaman," Arancibia said, grabbing a bundle of pamphlets. "How many do you have? I'd say about fifty."

"This is a meeting to discuss ideas," Aravena protested. "My party has a right to perform acts of propaganda. Revisionist methods won't silence us."

"You're quite right," Arancibia replied. "Isn't that so, comrades? Ideas should be discussed, absorbed and digested. We'll help you digest them. Take your pamphlets and roll them up into a ball, nice and small."

"Let me back in the meeting. Contradictions among the people can't be resolved by bullying."

"Don't be stubborn, roll them up," another of the brigade members said. They began to close in on him.

Feeling like a Christian in the Roman arena, Coco Aravena looked for help beyond the circle. He caught sight of Cacho Salinas and Lolo Garmendia, and was pleased to see they were wearing Young Socialist armbands. He called out to them.

"What's the matter, Chinaman?" Salinas shouted back. "Are you in trouble?"

"You know me, you know our differences are not irreconcilable. My party also belongs to the Nonaligned Movement, we believe in non-interference in the internal affairs of nations."

"Well, that's nice to know, asshole," Garmendia said. "So what's the problem?"

"There's no problem," Arancibia cut in. "What's happening is that our comrade here has to digest his ideas, and to do that he has to put them inside his body. You choose.

Either you eat them one by one down to the last pamphlet, or we stick them up your ass. That means you have two options: top or bottom."

The taste of mimeograph ink lingered for four months. Still laughing, Lucho Arancibia poured him a glass of wine.

Coco Aravena drank. The warmth of the wine made him forget that he was soaking wet, he grabbed a chicken thigh, and also burst into laughter.

"I ate all the pamphlets. For a long time my girlfriend said that kissing me was like kissing Gutenberg. Bastards."

"What the hell are you doing here, Coco?" Garmendia asked.

Oddly, Coco Aravena couldn't think of any screenplay this time. He simply told the story exactly as it had happened, and as he did so he realized that Concha and he had dug themselves into a hole it was difficult, if not impossible, to get out of. At the end of his story, he placed the revolver on the table.

"Are you absolutely sure the man died?" Garmendia insisted.

Aravena nodded, and with great economy of words told them about the blow received by the dead man, the size of the wound to his head, and the quantity of blood which he lost. There wasn't the slightest doubt.

"Your wife killed the specialist," Arancibia moaned.

"Lolo," Salinas said, "now that everything's fucked up again, please tell us what it is we were going to do. At least I'd like to know what kind of trouble I was about to get myself into. Tell us and then we can go. I'm freezing to death here."

Garmendia rubbed his bald head. He did not consider

himself even a moderate drinker, but he again poured himself some wine. "All right, but first let's decide what we're going to do with him," he said, indicating Coco Aravena, who was finishing off another chicken thigh.

"Easy," Salinas cried. "We take him to the back of the garage, tie him to a post, then take out our Kalashnikovs and shoot him. That's the traditional solution, isn't it?"

Aravena stopped eating, and commented that things weren't as bad as all that.

"First we have to set up a people's court," Arancibia said. "Charges and counter charges until the comrade makes the required self-criticism. I don't know if you thought of this, but the Chinaman has gotten his wife mixed up in this nasty business. The one lesson I've learned from the defeat is that we ourselves form a powerful sectarian fifth column. I suggest we invoke the spirit of the Asturian miners in '34."

"And you say the soldiers messed with your head," Garmendia said. "You're right, we're old and we're fucked. Let him stay."

Aravena threw a few more sticks on the fire and the four men sat down, unnaturally calm all of a sudden. The rain was still coming down thick and fast, but they didn't care about the cold, or the night, or the knowledge that on the other side of the door was a hostile city filled with the scars of what had once been.

Clutching his glass, Salinas recalled a weekend in Galicia, when things were already going quite badly with Matilde and he had used the excuse that he wanted to take the waters, in order to spend three days alone in Mondariz.

He arrived at sunset, settled in at the resort, couldn't get to sleep, and at dawn went out for a walk. A dense fog covered everything, you couldn't see more than a few feet in front of you, and he started walking straight toward a metal construction he could just about make out. It was a bridge over the river. The river itself was invisible, but you could hear the crystalline sound of water. Suddenly, he saw an old woman a few yards ahead of him. She was walking stooped over, and was dressed entirely in black. He felt afraid, but it was a vague, brief, temporary, fear. His reason told him that it was just an old Galician woman. He continued walking, and after half an hour realized, to his surprise, that he had not run into a single other person.

The fog was getting thicker as he climbed toward the town of Mondariz, or so he supposed, since just after the bridge he had seen a road sign indicating the direction to follow. He could hear the noise of his own steps on the paved path, regular steps that suddenly stopped being regular, interrupted as they were by the steps of one, two or more other walkers. The fog began to fill with the smell of still damp, recently felled firewood. He stopped, closed his eyes, breathed in, and recognized it as the smell of the little towns of Cautín, Cañete, and Carahue, lost in the thick fog of southern Chile. He must be delirious, he thought, he must be hallucinating. Opening his eyes, he saw Fredy Taberna walking in the fog and called out, "Fredy, brother, they killed you in the north, what are you doing in Galicia?" After Fredy came Sergio Leiva, carrying his inseparable guitar, and he called out to him, too. "Sergio, brother, they killed you in Santiago, what are you doing in Galicia?" Then came Lumi Videla, who had been killed in a military prison and her body thrown into the grounds of the Italian embassy. "Lumi, what are you doing in

Galicia?" None of them answered, although they were all walking with smiles on their faces.

Many others passed by, men and women he didn't know, but they were all his brothers and sisters in the fog. He was not afraid, nor was he surprised when he turned and started back to the resort. By the time he reached the end of the bridge, the sun was starting to break through the fog and he didn't have the least doubt that he was in Galicia, in Spain, having made the excuse of taking the waters as a way of stifling the chaos of feelings that was threatening to overwhelm him.

Nor did he have the slightest doubt that, for the defeated, life had turned into a fog bank, into the mist of those condemned to preserve the best of their memories, those few years from '68 to '73 when every day had been marked by a smile of the most militant optimism.

From then on, Cacho Salinas always remembered his dead with smiles on their faces. There was no screw-up, he told himself, that couldn't be overcome with a good laugh.

"Master," Salinas said, touching Garmendia's arm, "spill the beans."

"The specialist was just that: a specialist. He was a few years older than us, he must have been about seventy, something like that, and he was a strange teacher of many things we know without knowing that he, in his way, bequeathed them to us militants.

"I assume you all remember certain rules of living the underground life, keeping a look out for unusual vehicles on the street, always carrying a lot of tokens for public phones, never getting off at the same stop, those details you never find in books but which are passed on from one person to another. You probably also remember the first bank robberies, or the raid on the Portofino supermarket. Although committed by militants who hadn't the slightest experience, they were clean, perfectly executed, with no violence and no casualties. Well, the man who died was behind all of them. He didn't take part, he simply taught us how they were done. Some people called him The Shadow.

"In '71, the right decided to move currency out of the country illegally. The intention was to leave the country without dollars. A whole series of anonymous private banks were created, where they put the money before moving it to banks in Miami. Agents linked to the right bought dollars at much higher prices than those of the Central Bank or the exchange bureaus. The Americans had given them a blank check to ruin the country. On May 1, '71, I met the Shadow. He suddenly came up to me during a demonstration, took me by the arm, and said he wanted to talk to me about something. I followed him, and what he said astonished me. 'I've been watching you, you move well during the demonstration, you know what to look for, you establish the right boundaries. The fact that they allow you so close to the platform tells me you're one of the people in charge of security, and that means you're in the NLA. Take this envelope. In it, you'll find the address of a secret bank. Between the twelfth and the fifteenth of this month, there'll be almost a quarter of a million dollars there, ready to leave the country. You'll also find instructions in the envelope on how to seize that money. I'll give you two days to decide if you want to do it or not. If you decide not to, I'll pass the same information on to the Revolutionary Left Movement. I'll contact you the day after tomorrow, in the Café Santos at five in the afternoon.'

"I passed the information to the leadership of the NLA, and they ordered me to go to the appointment and say, yes, we'll do it. I went to the Café Santos, and found the Shadow drinking cocoa. We talked for about ten minutes, and when I indicated that I was about to leave, he told me to wait. 'I'll give you a present,' he said, 'I'll teach you how to get out of here without using the door.' The Café Santos was in a cellar, on the corner of Ahumada and Huérfanos. We went to the men's toilets, and opened a little window which led to a narrow passage. We went along it, through a hatchway, then down another, even narrower passage flanked by electric cables, gas pipes and waste pipes. This passage took us to a narrow metal door, with a frame that was also of metal. The edges of the frame, which came down to a fraction of an inch above the floor, were hollow. He put a finger inside the left edge and extracted a key tied to a spring, opened the door, and hid the key again. We entered a very dark space, where we could hear people panting at the height of sexual ecstasy. They were speaking English, Oh baby, the woman was saying, oh baby, the man was saying, porn movies don't have much dialogue. We were in a storeroom behind the screen of the Roxy movie house. We entered the auditorium, and slipped past some guys who were jerking off and didn't take any notice of us. We came out onto Calle Huérfanos through the entrance to a shopping arcade, and when I looked back I saw we were a hundred yards from the entrance to the Café Santos. 'The boy who's looking in the window of the pharmacy will go with you. Tell him that no one looks at a pharmacy for more than a couple of minutes. Bye, comrade, and good luck.'

"An operations group of the NLA seized those dollars

and put them in the Central Bank anonymously. I saw the Shadow three times, and three times we seized dollars from those secret banks. Every time we met, he would show me another escape route. He had escape routes all over the center of Santiago.

"The penultimate time I saw the Shadow was just before I went into exile. He was in front of the Identity Bureau, selling candy from a stall, and he told me he came there every day to observe the people who were getting passports. 'Good luck. I'll give you a piece of advice: take advantage of the time and study electronics, in the future war will be waged with wires and miniature things.'

"And I saw the Shadow for the last time thirty years later, about two months ago, as I was taking possession of my parents' house. How did he get in? I didn't ask him, the house had been officially empty for six months. He was sitting in the kitchen, reading and drinking cocoa from a thermos. He was a lot older than I remembered him. 'You haven't been looking after yourself, it was inevitable that you'd go bald, but you have to get rid of all that extra fat. Walk, walk every day, it's good for thinking and it burns the excess. I have something in hand at the moment. You remember those stashes of dollars? We missed one bank, the jackpot. I was keeping it as my own life insurance, though that's not important anymore, what matters is that the banker died, and in the best way he could have. On the eleventh of September '73, while celebrating the coup, he choked on a canapé, and it was good-bye Charlie. He was a mistrustful kind of fellow, so no one ever discovered the cache, and there are still half a million dollars there. The soldiers raised the floor, stripped the walls, took off the false ceiling, and still didn't find the hiding place. Until '75 it was a china shop, with exclusive rights to sell Lladró. You can imagine what soldiers can do in a china shop. They never found what they were looking for, even though they brought in metal detectors, infrared sights, heat detection apparatus. All to no avail. You want to know why? It was all my work, I designed the most secure hiding place. Until '80, the place was a beauty salon, then a travel agency, then a perfume shop, and now it's become a topless café. The windows are covered with a dark sheet, the café is always dimly lit, there are four or five girls who serve coffee and show their tits, plus a former army sergeant turned pimp who charges for the blow jobs the girls give in a private room. There are always between five and ten people there, maximum. If you want in, we have to do it on July 16 between six and eight in the morning.'"

"It's July 16 now," Coco Aravena remarked.

"The Shadow!" Cacho Salinas exclaimed. "I also met him just before going into exile, when, like so many others, I was running around the streets of Santiago trying to find someone who knew what was going on and could provide political direction. If my memory serves me well, I think it was in the Llano Supercaseaux, that huge park that ran parallel to the Gran Avenida. Arnoldo Camú, the NLA commander, had already been killed, but for some reason I kept going back to the meeting point we'd agreed on before the coup. I remember it clearly, in the same way I remember seeing and avoiding members of the security apparatus of the Left Revolutionary Movement who were coming up Calle Santa Fe, maybe heading for the same house where Miguel Enríquez died fighting like a tiger. Anyway, he came up to me, he was wearing blue overalls from the municipality of San Miguel and was sweeping one of the paths in the park. 'If I were you, comrade, I'd get out of here. I've seen you three days running and you're already far too well known. It doesn't matter to me what party you belong to, but if you care about morale something must be done. It's a time of defeat, a time for counting the dead, starting over again, and, above all, keeping up morale. The day after tomorrow, at exactly nine in the morning, there'll be a friendly operation. Are you in?'

"Breaking all the rules of security, I answered yes. There was something old and good about the guy, the kind of thing that impressed us in the old photos of the Russian revolution or the guys with beards entering Havana. He gave me an address and I went. The friendly operation took place on the corner of Santa Rosa and Sebastopol. I saw a number of well-known faces, comrades from the Communist Party, from the Revolutionary Left Movement, Socialists. We all looked at each other, not sure if we'd been lured into a trap. Then we saw a huge truck coming toward us, piled high with loaves of Ideal bread. When it reached the corner, it was rammed by a municipal van. The Shadow jumped out of the van, pointed a gun at the driver of the truck, and told us what he expected of us. We opened the rear door and began sharing the bread among the passers-by. I don't know if it was the Shadow or another comrade who said, 'We are the Resistance, take heart, comrades,' and soon we had a whole crowd of people taking the bread, giving us big warm hugs, and telling us to be careful. It all took about ten minutes and by the time the soldiers arrived there wasn't a soul on the street, or any bread, or any sign of the Shadow."

Coco Aravena was shaking his head disconsolately and clenching his fists. "It's my fault we killed the Shadow. I can't believe it, because I also took part in a friendly operation. After the military coup, I was confused and ashamed. I saw the bodies on the streets, and my Party was putting out documents talking about the errors of the popular government and blaming those who were dying for all the horror being heaped on our heads. One day, it must have been at the end of September, I found myself by pure chance in Barrascal, a working class district, and I immediately recognized various comrades from other parties. Everything happened very quickly. A tricycle passed in front of a Gasco truck, forcing it to stop, and the rider of the tricycle pointed . . . this same gun!" Coco Aravena cried, and the cry transformed his face into a mask of grief.

"And they gave out the gas cylinders in the name of the Resistance," Salinas concluded.

Lucho Arancibia poured more wine, stoked the fire, and then looked at the zinc roof. "The Shadow came here, too. When I got out of prison, my parents organized a symbolic funeral for my brother Juan. The garage had been closed for several years and the idea was to sell it. Many of our people came, neighbors, lifelong friends. That was how I met him, he was one of the many who showed his affection for my parents. He called me over, said that he had something personal to tell me, and we went into a corner, away from the others. 'Don't sell the garage, it may be useful for many things, for example to keep vigil over your brother Alberto when his body shows up. We'll meet again.' And we did. Several years later, in '82, he came back to the garage. 'You know about metals, soldering, mechanics. I need some devices capable of throwing a steel chain about 150 feet into the air. Leave the front door open tomorrow, and someone will bring the materials. Are you in?'

"I did it. I made some crossbows that fired harpoons with ropes on the end and then several yards of steel chain. I shit myself laughing, wept for joy, sang and danced the first time the Manuel Rodríguez Patriotic Front left half of Santiago without electricity. My harpoons flew over the high tension towers, and the chains fell on the cables and caused some monumental short circuits. And those who threw them were Young Communists, the sons of the dead, of the exiles, of the fucked-up people like me. Shit. Cacho, I told you that if I talked too much you should give me a slap."

The four men looked at each other. Fatter, older, bald or with graying beards, they still cast the shadow of what they were.

"Well, are we in?" Garmendia asked, and the four men clinked their glasses in the rainy Santiago night.

15

Inspector Crespo dropped Detective Bobadilla at her home and went back to the old building that housed the Department of Criminal Investigations. He was nervous, increasingly concerned that an armed, married man was at loose in the city.

He called Concepción García. In a sleepy voice, she informed him that her husband had not yet returned.

He looked at the clock on the wall. It was two in the morning, and the rain had not stopped. He remembered the old nightwatchmen who used to walk around the city, equipped with sticks, lanterns, and bunches of master keys, calling out the time and the weather.

"By the Holy Virgin Mary, it's two o'clock and raining."

He wondered when those municipal employees had disappeared, and if he really had seen them when he was a child, or if they were no more than the kind of strange certainty that had come about through listening inadvertently to the inventory of disappearances.

"What the hell were you planning, Pedrito?" he said out loud.

It crossed his mind that he should go down to the criminal records archive in the basement, where the files were generally illegible, rotted by damp or eaten by mice. He immediately dismissed the idea. He knew everything—and at the same time nothing—about Pedro Nolasco.

The inspector's neurons were working overtime. He remembered a photograph from the "armed and dangerous" files. A poor quality image taken in the general cemetery, which showed Nolasco at the age of thirty, the only mourner at a funeral. He was pulling a small cart with a coffin on it, draped in a black and red flag. The photograph was in black and white, but the inspector knew that the flag must have been red and black, since it was the funeral of the other Pedro Nolasco, the anarchist who, according to the files, had died from a gunshot wound fired from close range. Presumed suicide, even though the weapon was never found.

"Strange creatures, these anarchists," the inspector murmured.

There were no more men like that in Chile, they were part of the inventory of losses that sustained a false normality, the normality of two absolutely different countries coexisting in the same wretched geographical space. On one side, the prosperous country of the victors, situated in the western part of the city, the businessmen who greeted their politician neighbors with a smile, the women TV executives and boutique owners who drank cappuccinos on the terraces of shopping malls and chatted about the latest bargains to be had in Miami, and about how dirty Paris was, how chaotic Rome, how smelly Madrid, and, displaying their impeccable white teeth, asserted that there was nothing better than living in their little Chile. On the other hand there was the center of Santiago, where people walked with downcast eyes, intimidated by the video cameras that watched their every step and the policemen in their green vans with fenced windows and the security guards who kept an eye on them in banks and shops. And then there were the southern, northern and western districts, haunted by the despair of precarious employment and overrun by juvenile delinquents who, after frying their brains with pasta base, turned into baby-faced psychopaths.

"There are no more anarchists," the inspector sighed.

The last one had died in 1990. A handsome old man with a long white beard who always wore workers' overalls and looked like Leo Tolstoy's twin brother. His name was Clotario Blest, anarcho-syndicalist, pacifist, vegetarian, macrobiotic, an ecologist when no one knew the meaning of the word, and founder of the United Confederation of Workers, the biggest and best-organized trade union body in Latin America.

Inspector Crespo remembered seeing him at demonstrations against the dictatorship, always at the front, demanding news of the thousands of men and women who had disappeared, and being dragged away by strapping police officers who merely accentuated the strength emanating from his weak body. Always in the frontline.

Clotario Blest was no longer around, and neither was the United Confederation of Workers. They were both part of the inventory of losses.

"What the hell were you planning, Pedrito?" he said again in a low voice, and at that moment glanced at the calendar on his desk.

July 16. He leaped to his feet, went to the central computer and searched for bank robberies.

On July 16, 1925, Pedrito's grandfather, together with three Spanish anarchists, had raided the Matadero branch of the Bank of Chile.

Inspector Crespo liked coincidences because life was full of them. You simply had to accept them in silence, they couldn't be used to justify taking preventive measures, so he did what any police officer struck by a coincidence would do: nothing.

He took off his shoes, put his feet up on the desk, closed his eyes and murmured, "Alright, Pedrito, if what you were going to do was a lone act, there's nothing to worry about, but if you had accomplices, let them at least do it the way you would have done and we'll be fine."

16.

It was five in the morning and still raining, although more lightly now. The four men in the garage were getting ready to head out. Lolo Garmendia took charge of the revolver, checked that the six .38 special caliber bullets were in the cylinder and put the weapon away. Lucho Arancibia put a mallet and a chisel in a sports bag. Coco Aravena was still fighting the unrepentant screenwriter inside him, and temporarily lost the fight.

"Guys, although you may not think so, I know something about these things. From what Lolo said, it won't be difficult to get in. Obviously, at six in the morning, the alarms won't be on, so they won't be set off when people move about in the arcade. That's clear, but inside there may be cameras, microphones, so I suggest we cover the bottom halves of our faces with handkerchiefs, and that, when we talk to each other, we don't use our real names. Lolo can be Mr. Black, Cacho, Mr. Brown, Lucho, Mr. Red, and I—"

"The name of the movie is *Reservoir Dogs*," Salinas said, cutting him short. "Were you born like this?"

"Red," Arancibia said. "Like John Reed, the author of *Ten Days That Shook the World*. He was a great American comrade, who's buried in the Kremlin, next to Lenin. But I've never heard about these others, Black and Brown. There are a lot of gaps in my political education."

"Do you need a slap?" Salinas asked.

It was 5.10 a.m. when they walked out onto Calle Matucana. The rain was lighter now, but hadn't stopped. They agreed that they would go to the Plaza de Armas in two taxis and meet up again by the monument to Valdivia. Garmendia and Arancibia got in the first taxi, Salinas and Aravena in the second.

At 5.40, they met at the agreed place. There were already a fair number of people hurrying across the Plaza de Armas, walking hunched over in a futile attempt not to get too wet, even those who carried umbrellas. The mounted conquistador glistened in the rain. The statue cried out for a higher base to exaggerate the rider's gesture, but, just as an architect had removed the steps of the cathedral, leaving the nave at street level, low, squat and irrevocably ugly, they had put Pedro de Valdivia on such a low base that he simply looked like a guy on a horse who kept getting in the way of the pedestrians.

"You remember when we were students?" Coco Aravena asked. He walked around to the back of the monument, climbed on the base, and gave the horse's magnificent testicles a loud kiss.

"You really were born like that," Salinas commented.

"The Chinaman's right," Arancibia said. "It's been scientifically proved that kissing the horses' balls brings luck." And he, too, placed his lips on the bronze testicles.

The two others followed suit.

At 5:55 they entered the San Antonio arcade by the entrance on Calle Merced. The café with its windows covered by a thick black curtain was called The Happy Dragon and was located directly opposite the bookstore *Le Monde diplomatique*. Garmendia remembered the

Shadow's words: it's a quiet place, at that early-morning hour no one hangs around outside a bookstore, this is Santiago after all.

Using the chisel as a lever, Lucho Arancibia prized open the padlock on the shutter with its metal rhomboids. They raised the shutter, forced open the aluminum and glass door, again with the chisel, then lowered the shutter, and Garmendia replaced the broken padlock with another similar one.

The smell inside The Happy Dragon was a mixture of mildew and coffee. The room measured no more than 140 square feet. There were five high stools lined up in front of the counter. At one end was the cash register, and behind it a Cimbali coffee machine and a rack with cups and saucers, and behind that a narrow private room furnished with a plastic couch half covered by the red miniskirts belonging to the girls who worked there.

"So far, so good," Garmendia said.

"Shall I make coffee?" Aravena whispered.

"God, you really are sick," Salinas murmured.

"Coffee wouldn't be a bad idea," Arancibia observed. "And if the Chinaman's offering . . ."

"Let him make coffee," Garmendia said. "Carry on talking. Keep it low, but talk. I have to think like the Shadow now and I can't think if I'm tense."

Coco Aravena jumped on the platform behind the counter. Because of its height, his bottom was in full view of his comrades. He started the coffee machine and made four cups. Garmendia moved away to the end of the counter and looked closely at the wall.

"Keep talking," he ordered.

"How's the coffee?" Aravena asked.

"Why don't you put on one of those skirts from the next room?" Arancibia asked sarcastically.

"This coffee's shit, but it's not your fault," Salinas said. "No one drinks coffee in Chile, we never had a coffee culture, and by the sixties this lack of a coffee culture had become a national trauma. Every Chilean who traveled to Europe came back talking about the coffee they were served in France or Italy, and things got worse when those who came back from Argentina commented on how good the coffee was in the coffee and cake shops in Buenos Aires. Here we continued drinking coffee made from figs, from beetroot, from everything except coffee. In the mid-Sixties, Nescafé came along, and a bourgeois bastard named Márquez De La Plata invented the national substitute, Sicafé, which was also complete shit. At the end of the Sixties, a daring entrepreneur decided to create a uniquely Chilean coffee culture, and opened the first Café Haiti on Calle Almuhada. It wouldn't have cost him much to use good coffee, roasted by people who knew what they were doing, but no, he used shit coffee, but in return he designed the café in a special way: he equipped it with an elevated platform behind the counter, hired working-class girls who had the kind of looks that appealed to the majority of men, because most men are, and will always be, attracted to big girls with big tits and asses, dressed them in miniskirts that took your breath away and got them to serve coffee, shit coffee again, but no one cared about the taste or if they burned their mouths, so long as it was served by these big, sexy girls who showed their thighs and had a tendency to drop spoons on the floor so they could show their asses when they picked them up. From that moment, we all became addicted to coffee served by girls in miniskirts. The Haiti opened more branches in the center. There wasn't a single civil servant, judge, deputy or notary who didn't dream about the girls who served coffee in miniskirts. Then he opened the São Paulo, which didn't just have girls in miniskirts, but plunging necklines, too. Who doesn't remember those girls leaning over the coffee cups, stirring the sugar and asking, Do you take milk? while the customers broke out in a sweat at the view of that more than generous cleavage. Then, comrades, the dictatorship arrived, and the free market, and we ended up with topless cafés like this one, which, believe me, we are raiding. And then there were cafés with happy hours where the girls stripped naked to keep the old fools happy. As we know, the free market is sacrosanct, so the Catholic morality of Chile had no difficulty in accepting the idea of working class girls prostituting themselves. And the coffee was still complete shit."

"Amen," Lucho Arancibia said.

"Silence," Garmendia ordered. "The extractor fan is recent, no more than ten years old. Since this building dates from the 1930s, the old ventilation system must be in a corner near a pillar." He pointed toward the ceiling. "Lucho, start there."

Mallet in hand, Arancibia started to chip away at the wall; the layer of plaster fell easily, revealing the color of bricks behind. Garmendia examined it.

"An intelligent man, the Shadow. These bricks are from the seventies. That's why the soldiers didn't find the entrance to the treasure: he covered the original wall with this false wall of bricks. Carry on, Lucho."

Arancibia carried on. By 7.15 a.m. he had found the entrance to an air vent. He put in, first his hand, then his arm, and a number of mummified rats fell out. Then, in a cloud of dust, he took out a suitcase wrapped in plastic.

The four men left The Happy Dragon at 7:30, lowered the metal shutter, and locked it with the padlock.

A man who was looking down at the ground asked them if the café was already open.

"Not yet," Arancibia replied. "At eight. The girls are getting ready."

They left the arcade by the exit on Calle San Antonio. They kept walking, surrounded by people hunched in the rain, as far as La Alameda, and on Ahumada they disappeared into the subway.

17

Concepción García was looking at her husband incredulously. They had met at the door of the building as she was coming out, carrying a bag with three changes of underwear, toiletries, and a copy of *Berlin Alexanderplatz*. Before leaving Berlin she had promised herself that she would read Alfred Döblin's novel in German, that thick book would keep her close to her lost city, and a long way from the prison to which she was sure to be sentenced for many years.

"Concha," he had said, "where are you going so early?"

"To give myself up. The police know everything and I confessed my guilt."

"Your guilt? Conchita, come back, let's talk, and together we'll decide what to say."

"No, Coco. I don't want any more stories, any more movies. I don't want any more classics of anything."

That was when she had gotten her first surprise. Her husband had hugged her, kissed her on the lips and the eyes, and said a few words that were totally out of keeping with the Coco Aravena she had known all her life:

"Let's go together, Conchita. And together we'll tell the whole truth."

Inspector Crespo scratched his beard. He wondered why

it grew more when he stayed up all the night than it did when he slept.

"Adelita, could you leave us alone for a few minutes, please?"

Detective Bobadilla went out and the inspector cursed the hour when he had quit smoking.

"All right, Señor Aravena. We've established that, after a passionate exchange of views about your laziness, depression, disillusionment, lack of ambition, contempt for work and possibly lack of decency, the lady lost her temper and threw some things out the window without noticing that, through a piece of bad luck, a man who was walking along the street was hit by a phonograph and immediately died. We've also established that, in your desperation, you invented a somewhat grotesque ploy to protect her, making a false report of a robbery with the intention of putting the blame on a third party."

"That's right, officer. And once again I insist that the fault is entirely mine. What happened is all down to me and the way I behaved. So I beg you to put me on trial. I'm ready to serve whatever sentence is imposed on me."

"Not so fast. You also claim to be completely ignorant of the dead man's identity."

"I'd never seen him before in my life. I offer voluntarily to take a lie detector test or be given pentothal injections."

"It's obvious you're a film buff. Let's see. Once again, why did you take the dead man's gun, why did you hide it, and why did you go out later carrying it with you?"

"I don't know why I took it. It was an impulse. I thought maybe I could sell it."

Not too implausible, the inspector thought, we all carry

a little thief inside us. People steal from supermarkets for the pure adventure of doing so.

"But why did you go out again with the gun? What were you planning to do?"

"I don't know that either. I admit that I had the idea of doing something, robbing a shop, a bank, a gas station. But I didn't do it."

Now, the inspector thought, I'll ask you the crucial question and if you mention in your answer that you're a coward, I've got you, you idiot.

"Why didn't you do it? After all, you had a gun."

"Because I don't know how it's done. In movies it never rains like this, the attackers are never soaking wet and dying of cold. And as if that wasn't enough, I don't know how to use a gun, I've never fired a shot in my life. I sat down in a park, to think, and didn't even do that. Please, let my wife go. You can do whatever you like with me. I've come to give myself up."

The worst thing about this job, the inspector thought, is the necessity to see the thin line that separates the criminal from the victim of chance. They don't teach that in the police academy. If this guy had come here without the revolver, claiming that he had thrown it in the river or in a garbage can, even at the risk of being wrong, I wouldn't have believed him.

The inspector took the revolver, saw that it was extremely well lubricated, and smelled the cylinder. It had the unmistakable almond smell of Remington oil, which they had stopped selling in the 1970s and replaced with silicon solutions. Then he swung out the cylinder and looked through the barrel. The striations showed imperfections possibly caused by the friction of poor quality bullets, homemade bullets produced clandestinely, like the ones he had taken out of the cylinder: old bullets of pure lead, which, when they were fired, would leave traces of scum in the tiny grooves he could easily see in the striations, rendering the weapon unusable and quite risky to whoever fired it.

"Señor Aravena, Señora Aravena, you can both go."

Concepción García made a surprised gesture, and her husband seemed about to open his mouth, but the inspector pointed to the door.

He watched them go out hand in hand. He yawned and called Detective Bobadilla back into the room.

"Adelita, would you do me the honor of having breakfast with me? Let's go to La Selecta."

In silence, they walked the three blocks separating them from the huge bakery and café opposite the central market. There, they sat down at a table on the third floor, and the inspector ordered two complete breakfasts, with fried eggs, papaya juice, and newly-baked flat bread.

"Do you have something to tell me, inspector?" Detective Bobadilla asked.

"Adelita, you and I both know things that can't be talked about: investigations shelved on orders from above, criminals released because incriminating evidence went missing, murderers and violators of every human right allowed to walk free and rewarded with jobs in big business or in the diplomatic corps. The only crime those two committed was to come back to Chile. What happened was a tragic coincidence, an accident, nothing more. We both know how justice works in our country. They would have spent months, even years, in jail, until a judge sentenced them to pay a ridiculous fine."

"What you did wasn't very orthodox."

"No, it isn't. You're quite right. But I try to be fair, although a police officer should limit himself to arresting suspects. As I was talking with them, I checked Pedrito's gun. It was an old weapon, with the striations on the barrel visibly damaged. I think that, by chance, they did him a favor. If Pedrito had been planning to use that revolver, it would have blown up in his hands after two shots, and splinters somehow always go for the eyes. Can you imagine a blind anarchist?"

"Do you know something, inspector? When I was about to get my detective's badge, they took us from the academy to Villa Grimaldi for an exercise in searching for prints. I had no idea that house existed, or what it was, or the people who'd been tortured there, or murdered, or made to disappear. I don't believe in ghosts or auras, but there was a terrible feeling about the place that made me nauseous. After a while, I walked away from my group, and found myself listening to a woman who was telling other people that she had been there. She was a frail but beautiful woman, later I discovered she was a writer, and she was talking about the terrible things she had endured together with many other women prisoners. The strange thing is that there was no resentment in her voice. Pain, yes, but a pain free of hatred, a pain full of dignity, which I found beautiful, having grown up during the dictatorship hearing messages of hate every day. I went up to her and said: I'm a police officer, for myself and on behalf of the institution I represent I want to ask your forgiveness for all you suffered, and I swear to you it will never happen again. She looked at me sweetly, asked how old I was and, when I told her I was born in 1973, she hugged me and said, you're not to blame, your hands are clean. I'm with you, inspector."

"It's paradoxical, Adelita. Yours is the first generation of police officers capable of giving some dignity to what we do, and possibly the last. Very soon they'll announce that the police have been privatized, and everything you believe in will be left in the hands of mercenaries."

The old inspector and the young detective looked in each other's eyes. What they saw was what crime reporters and dispensers of medals call the satisfaction of a job well done, but which in reality is the pride of saying "I'm in" and following it up.

18.

*D*ear *Comrade, if you are reading this letter written some years ago, it's likely you found it where I left it the last time I entered the place where the treasure is hidden to make sure that everything was still safe and to take out a few dollars, not many, just enough to answer the needs of a solitary fighter and confirmed bachelor. I won't go into details about how I did it, but if you imagine being disguised as a construction worker, you're on the right track.*

If we were together a few hours ago, then you know that I am dead. They'll say on the news that an old man shot himself in a place of dubious morality, and I imagine you'll have a lot of questions.

I come from a long line of suicides, I decided freely when to end my days because I am an anarchist. Paul Lafargue (read The Right to Be Lazy*) and Laura Marx committed suicide together to avoid the humiliation of old age. In Chile, the father of the workers' movement, Luis Emilio Recabarren, killed himself when he realized that, by incorporating into the Communist movement the work of so many, work which had cost so many lives, he had sacrificed the libertarian roots of the best ideas and subjected them to the will of those who were ready to sacrifice freedom for power. Freedom is a state of grace, but only if you're free* *when you fight for it. My paternal grandfather was one of the first Chilean anarchists, a printer who taught me to read Cervantes and Tolstoy and who participated anonymously in many acts against the powers that be. One day he made the supreme decision to say farewell to life in order not to be an obstacle in my path. He used the same revolver that I have now used to stop being a man and set off on the path of shadows.*

We anarchists die without fuss, we don't go in for propaganda. If you are reading this letter it's July 16 and it's after nine in the morning, which means the police will have received a letter with a detailed sketch of the Happy Dragon. They'll take away the counter, get rid of the floor tiles, and find a hatchway which leads to a treasure box. There is no money in it, but there are some papers with the codes to various Swiss bank accounts opened between 1974 and 1980. The owners, all retired military men, will have to account for where the money came from. As it happens, there's also a notebook in that box that gives a full account of the origin of that money, and of how the booty was divided up: houses that had belonged to people who were murdered, vehicles received in return for a safe conduct to leave the country, looted art objects sold in prestigious European galleries, shares given in exchange for safe conducts out of the torture centers, jewelry accepted in the name of "national reconstruction," and, above all, bribes. In 1995, a number of photocopies were sent anonymously to the government: photocopies of checks issued by the army to a son of the dictator in the amount of three million dollars, a pittance compared with what the police will find today. It was a test: I wanted to know if the newly restored Chilean democracy could be trusted. We all know the answer to that: Pinochet sent troops into the streets and it was as if those checks had never existed.

It's very satisfying to assume that, as you read this letter, my body will still be lying in this wretched place, or perhaps they'll already have moved me to the morgue in order to let the police get on with their job.

You will wonder why I did it. A man knows when he has reached the end of his road: the body gives warning signs, that wonderful mechanism that keeps you intelligent and alert starts to fail, your memory does everything possible to save you and embellishes what you'd prefer to remember objectively. Never trust memory, because it's always on our side. It embellishes the ugly, sweetens the bitter, casts light where there was only shadow. Memory always tends toward fiction.

I was going to die soon anyway. That was why I took the revolver, I've never fired it in my life, and this act had to be clean, silent, like all those in which I have participated. The one shot I fired in my life had to be a homage to myself.

You will also wonder why I chose you. The answer is quite simple. I watched you during a demonstration. You were afraid, but you accepted your fear, you didn't hide from it. Brave people don't exist, only people who agree to go hand to hand with their fear.

If nothing has upset my plans, you will be with the men who have joined us. In the suitcase there is almost half a million dollars in fifty- and hundred-dollar bills. You need to be careful, these bills were issued before 1974. Only change as much as you need to get you out of financial difficulty, don't change your lifestyle conspicuously. I suggest a journey to the south, changing small quantities in every town. Later you could go abroad—it's possible to take up to ten thou-

sand out of the country legally. Don't trust banks, keep the money, but never forget that the great paradox of having a fortune is that it brings problems with it.

Finally, you may wonder why I was so insistent that this had to be done today, July 16. It has a personal significance for me.

If no one reads this letter, if I am writing in vain and life spoiled my plans, so be it. But if these words fall into the hands of some construction worker who's demolishing or renovating the building, then I say, take advantage, comrade.

EPILOGUE

They say that at the exit from the San Antonio arcade a blind man was singing: *Where my mother lives, they say, the water and the wind both say, they saw the guerrillas pass that way.*

They say that an inspector and a young female detective from the Criminal Investigation Department were the first people to reach the Happy Dragon.

They say that by ten in the morning, the five girls who worked in the café were already in their red miniskirts, and the former sergeant turned pimp was sweeping up bits of fallen plaster and looking in astonishment at the hole that had been made in a corner of the room very close to the ceiling.

They say that a few minutes later, more police officers arrived, armed with pickaxes and shovels, took the counter and the coffee machine away from the arcade, and forced the girls to leave, making sure they first covered themselves against the July cold.

They say that the inspector received an urgent call from higher up, ordering him to seal off the scene of the crime and avoid touching anything, until someone of overriding authority arrived.

They say that the inspector crossed the arcade, entered the bookstore *Le Monde diplomatique*, and asked if they had a press directory.

They say that the young female detective called all the newspapers, radio stations, and TV channels, and that very soon the whole place was awash with microphones, cameras, lights, tape recorders, and people hurriedly taking notes.

They say that by the time those from higher up arrived, the inspector was reading aloud the contents of an account book, a book that contained some well-known names and some quite alarming figures.

They say that by noon on that July 16 it had stopped raining over Santiago.

About the Author

Born in Chile in 1949, Luis Sepúlveda left his native country after years of political activism lead to his incarceration under Augusto Pinochet's regime. Following his initial career as a poet he received literary acclaim in 1989 with his novel *The Old Man Who Read Love Stories*. He lives in Spain.

Carmine Abate
Between Two Seas
"A moving portrayal of generational continuity."
—*Kirkus*
224 pp • $14.95 • 978-1-933372-40-2

Salwa Al Neimi
The Proof of the Honey
"Al Neimi announces the end of a taboo in the Arab world:
that of *sex!*"
—*Reuters*
144 pp • $15.00 • 978-1-933372-68-6

Alberto Angela
A Day in the Life of Ancient Rome
"Fascinating and accessible."
—*Il Giornale*
392 pp • $16.00 • 978-1-933372-71-6

Muriel Barbery
The Elegance of the Hedgehog
"Gently satirical, exceptionally winning and inevitably bittersweet."
—Michael Dirda, *The Washington Post*
336 pp • $15.00 • 978-1-933372-60-0

Gourmet Rhapsody
"In the pages of this book, Barbery shows off her finest gift: lightness."
—*La Repubblica*
176 pp • $15.00 • 978-1-933372-95-2

Stefano Benni
Margherita Dolce Vita
"A modern fable...hilarious social commentary."—*People*
240 pp • $14.95 • 978-1-933372-20-4

Timeskipper
"Benni again unveils his Italian brand of magical realism."
—*Library Journal*
400 pp • $16.95 • 978-1-933372-44-0

Romano Bilenchi
The Chill
120 pp • $15.00 • 978-1-933372-90-7

Massimo Carlotto
The Goodbye Kiss
"A masterpiece of Italian noir."
—*Globe and Mail*
160 pp • $14.95 • 978-1-933372-05-1

Death's Dark Abyss
"A remarkable study of corruption and redemption."
—*Kirkus* (starred review)
160 pp • $14.95 • 978-1-933372-18-1

The Fugitive
"[Carlotto is] the reigning king of Mediterranean noir."
—*The Boston Phoenix*
176 pp • $14.95 • 978-1-933372-25-9

(with Marco Videtta)
Poisonville
"The business world as described by Carlotto and Videtta
in *Poisonville* is frightening as hell."
—*La Repubblica*
224 pp • $15.00 • 978-1-933372-91-4

Francisco Coloane
Tierra del Fuego
"Coloane is the Jack London of our times."—Alvaro Mutis
192 pp • $14.95 • 978-1-933372-63-1

Giancarlo De Cataldo
The Father and the Foreigner
"A slim but touching noir novel from one of Italy's best writers
in the genre."—*Quaderni Noir*
144 pp • $15.00 • 978-1-933372-72-3

Shashi Deshpande
The Dark Holds No Terrors
"[Deshpande is] an extremely talented storyteller."—*Hindustan Times*
272 pp • $15.00 • 978-1-933372-67-9

Helmut Dubiel
Deep In the Brain: Living with Parkinson's Disease
"A book that begs reflection."—*Die Zeit*
144 pp • $15.00 • 978-1-933372-70-9

Steve Erickson
Zeroville
"A funny, disturbing, daring and demanding novel—Erickson's best."
—*The New York Times Book Review*
352 pp • $14.95 • 978-1-933372-39-6

Elena Ferrante
The Days of Abandonment
"The raging, torrential voice of [this] author is something rare."
—*The New York Times*
192 pp • $14.95 • 978-1-933372-00-6

Troubling Love
"Ferrante's polished language belies the rawness of her imagery."
—*The New Yorker*
144 pp • $14.95 • 978-1-933372-16-7

The Lost Daughter
"So refined, almost translucent."—*The Boston Globe*
144 pp • $14.95 • 978-1-933372-42-6

Jane Gardam
Old Filth
"Old Filth belongs in the Dickensian pantheon of memorable characters."
—*The New York Times Book Review*
304 pp • $14.95 • 978-1-933372-13-6

The Queen of the Tambourine
"A truly superb and moving novel."—*The Boston Globe*
272 pp • $14.95 • 978-1-933372-36-5

The People on Privilege Hill
"Engrossing stories of hilarity and heartbreak."—*Seattle Times*
208 pp • $15.95 • 978-1-933372-56-3

The Man in the Wooden Hat
"Here is a writer who delivers the world we live in…with memorable and
moving skill."—*The Boston Globe*
240 pp • $15.00 • 978-1-933372-89-1

Alicia Giménez-Bartlett
Dog Day
"Delicado and Garzón prove to be one of the more engaging sleuth teams
to debut in a long time."—*The Washington Post*
320 pp • $14.95 • 978-1-933372-14-3

Prime Time Suspect
"A gripping police procedural."—*The Washington Post*
320 pp • $14.95 • 978-1-933372-31-0

Death Rites
"Petra is developing into a good cop, and her earnest efforts to assert her
authority…are worth cheering."—*The New York Times*
304 pp • $16.95 • 978-1-933372-54-9

Katharina Hacker
The Have-Nots
"Hacker's prose soars."—*Publishers Weekly*
352 pp • $14.95 • 978-1-933372-41-9

Patrick Hamilton
Hangover Square
"Patrick Hamilton's novels are dark tunnels of misery, loneliness, deceit, and sexual obsession."—*New York Review of Books*
336 pp • $14.95 • 978-1-933372-06-

James Hamilton-Paterson
Cooking with Fernet Branca
"Irresistible!"—*The Washington Post*
288 pp • $14.95 • 978-1-933372-01-3

Amazing Disgrace
"It's loads of fun, light and dazzling as a peacock feather."
—*New York Magazine*
352 pp • $14.95 • 978-1-933372-19-8

Rancid Pansies
"Campy comic saga about hack writer and self-styled 'culinary genius' Gerald Samper."—*Seattle Times*
288 pp • $15.95 • 978-1-933372-62-4

Seven-Tenths: The Sea and Its Thresholds
"The kind of book that, were he alive now, Shelley might have written."
—*Charles Spawson*
416 pp • $16.00 • 978-1-933372-69-3

Alfred Hayes
The Girl on the Via Flaminia
"Immensely readable."—*The New York Times*
164 pp • $14.95 • 978-1-933372-24-2

Jean-Claude Izzo
Total Chaos
"Izzo's Marseilles is ravishing."—*Globe and Mail*
256 pp • $14.95 • 978-1-933372-04-4

Chourmo
"A bitter, sad and tender salute to a place equally impossible to love or leave."—*Kirkus* (starred review)
256 pp • $14.95 • 978-1-933372-17-4

Solea
"[Izzo is] a talented writer who draws from the deep, dark well of noir."
—*The Washington Post*
208 pp • $14.95 • 978-1-933372-30-3

The Lost Sailors
"Izzo digs deep into what makes men weep."—*Time Out New York*
272 pp • $14.95 • 978-1-933372-35-8

A Sun for the Dying
"Beautiful, like a black sun, tragic and desperate."—*Le Point*
224 pp • $15.00 • 978-1-933372-59-4

Gail Jones
Sorry
"Jones's gift for conjuring place and mood rarely falters."
—*Times Literary Supplement*
240 pp • $15.95 • 978-1-933372-55-6

Matthew F. Jones
Boot Tracks
"A gritty action tale."—*The Philadelphia Inquirer*
208 pp • $14.95 • 978-1-933372-11-2

Ioanna Karystiani
The Jasmine Isle
"A modern Greek tragedy about love foredoomed and family life."
—Kirkus
288 pp • $14.95 • 978-1-933372-10-5

Swell
"Karystiani movingly pays homage to the sea and those who live from it."
—La Repubblica
256 pp • $15.00 • 978-1-933372-98-3

Gene Kerrigan
The Midnight Choir
"The lethal precision of his closing punches leave quite a lasting mark."
—Entertainment Weekly
368 pp • $14.95 • 978-1-933372-26-6

Little Criminals
"A great story...relentless and brilliant."*—Roddy Doyle*
352 pp • $16.95 • 978-1-933372-43-3

Peter Kocan
Fresh Fields
"A stark, harrowing, yet deeply courageous work of immense power and magnitude."*—Quadrant*
304 pp • $14.95 • 978-1-933372-29-7

The Treatment and the Cure
"Kocan tells this story with grace and humor."*—Publishers Weekly*
256 pp • $15.95 • 978-1-933372-45-7